Operation Family

SEALed for You

Marissa Dobson

Published by Sunshine Press
Printed in the United States of America
ISBN-13: 978-1-939978-54-7

Dedication

To all the men and woman in the military who serve our country. To their families who serve in their own way, waiting for them, and supporting them through thick and thin.

Contents

The soldier above all others prays for peace, for it is the soldier who must suffer and bear the deepest wounds and scars of war. ~ Douglas MacArthur

Navy SEAL Lieutenant Commander Mac García spent twenty years in the military but had no plans to retire. He didn't know what his life would be like without the SEALs, and through the years he saw the worst in the world. He'd be damned if he'd see another attack on American soil. Arriving home, he's faced with a whole different obstacle—twin toddlers. As the only family left to these little girls, he has to figure out what the next step in his life will be and how he'll manage raising two children.

A knock at Nicole Ryan's door delivers the news of a friend's death, and now she's alone to care for the twins until their guardian arrives. As their nanny since they were born, she can't picture being separated from them, let alone seeing them head to the other side of the United States. She'll fight for the right to keep the girls, because she doesn't know how else to deal with the loss of their father, and she can't bear losing them too.

Can two people from different walks of life come together to build a strong family for the twins? Or will destiny make them lose everything they hold dear?

Chapter One

Navy SEAL Lieutenant Commander Mac García leaned back against the hard airport lounge chair, his eyes fluttering shut with exhaustion. Any hope of catching a few hours of sleep before takeoff was destroyed by the crying baby two seats over. Lights were strung around the airport, with Christmas trees throughout the terminal, and shops hung their seasonal items in the window calling to the travelers. Christmas was upon them, adding to the haste, and everyone rushed to their gates or baggage claim to get their holiday celebrations underway. He was sure the decorations were supposed to add to the joy of the season, but to him it was just depressing. There was no one waiting for him to get home from his latest mission and no one to spend the holidays with. His life was completely dedicated to SEAL Team Two; his days revolved around the squad of men serving under him.

At thirty-nine, he had put in his twenty years in the service and had no plans to retire. He didn't know what his life would consist of if it wasn't filled with training, missions, and the dreaded paperwork that came with leading the squad. No, he was suited for the military and would stay a SEAL until he couldn't keep up with the younger men.

He'd do his part in keeping the country safe from the dangers most didn't want to think of. On missions he saw the worst of the world, and he'd be damned if he saw another attack on America soil.

The baby's wails stiffened every muscle in his body, until he was as tight as a rubber band stretched to its limit. He rolled his neck and tried to ease the tension with no luck. Instead of sitting there trying to get a few hours of sleep before his plane took off, he rose, and tossed his duffle bag over his shoulder. The terminal was too busy for him to make it far without having to weave between other travelers, but he didn't need to go far. Anywhere else he managed to go there seemed to be some excitement. If it wasn't a baby crying, it was children playing, people on their cell phones, or worse, couples in love.

The sweet lovey-dovey couple in the corner made his stomach churn. They were one of the reasons he fought to keep this country safe, but being surrounded by it brought home the fact that he was alone. There would be no one waiting for him when he returned to Virginia. Not even the team he'd sent on ahead so they could enjoy the holiday celebrations with their families while he wrapped up a few additional details.

Damn, I need a beer and a good nights' sleep. Everything will look better in the morning, or at the very least when the fucking holidays are over.

"Daddy, Daddy!" A little boy no older than three sprinted toward him.

His gaze darted around in search of the boy's parents. In this day and age, how parents let their children go unattended surprised him. Some just didn't care and those were the ones who truly frightened him. Realizing the boy was alone, he dropped his bag, and knelt. "Hey, little man. Where's your mommy?"

"Daddy!" He wrapped his little arms around Mac's neck and clung as if his life depended on it.

"Christopher." A woman's frantic voice cut through the crowd.

He glanced in the direction that the voice had come from and there in the midst of the crowd a woman with a stroller making her way across the airport. Her frantic gaze searched the crowd, clearly terrified as she looked for her son.

"Looks like your mommy found us." He held tight to the boy, making sure he didn't slip out of his grasp and start running down the terminal again. "Ma'am."

"There you are, Christopher. What did I tell you about staying with me?" She knelt down and drew her son into her arms. "I'm sorry."

"Mommy, I found Daddy." The little boy tried to wiggle from her grasp but she held tight.

"No, sweetie. We've got to take an airplane trip to Virginia before we see Daddy." The woman stood, keeping hold of her son's hand. She looked at Mac. "I'm sorry. He's excited to see his father. I guess with the uniform he thought..."

"It's all right, ma'am. You seem to have your hands full. Can I help you to your gate?" With the shoulder bag, diaper bag, and two kids he wasn't sure how she had managed to get this far.

"It would appear I'm here." She nodded to the gate he had just stepped away from. "We were visiting my family for Thanksgiving and planned to stay through Christmas when I received word my husband was injured in the line of duty. He'll be arriving in Virginia tomorrow, so we're rushing to get home. Christopher is just so excited to see his father."

"I can tell." Mac ruffled the boy's sandy brown hair. "I'm sorry about your husband. I hope he'll be okay." His stomach roiled again. Another soldier whose life had been changed by the senseless act of war. Too many of his fellow warriors were killed in action, and even more had injures both physical and mental that would forever change their lives. He could only hope the woman's husband hadn't sustained too bad of injuries, and that he'd recover to be an active parent in his children's lives.

"My husband's vehicle was hit by an IED and he was badly burned. Thankfully he'll survive." The cries of the infant in the stroller tore through the terminal, and the mother gently rocked the stroller trying to calm her.

"Here, let me help you over to the chairs." Without waiting for her to agree, he picked up the bags she'd dropped when she hugged her son and took hold of the little boy's hand. "Would you like to sit by the window and watch the planes take off?"

"Can we?" Christopher bounced with excitement.

Crossing the distance to the row of seats by the window, Mac noted how easy children were to amuse. "Ma'am, I'm Lieutenant Commander Mac García, Navy SEAL."

"I appreciate your help, Commander. I'm Shelly James." She lifted her son onto the chair and turned back to him. "You don't need to stay. I can manage."

"Ma'am, military wives are a breed all their own. They have the strength and courage of their men tenfold. So I have no doubt you'd manage, but this is my gate as well. If you don't mind I'd gladly see you on board and settled with the children."

"Thank you." She lifted the baby out of the stroller, gently cradling her. "I'd like to apologize for Christopher's behavior. He knows that when his dad has been away on a deployment he'll be in uniform when he returns. He has a picture of his dad in uniform by his bed. It's the last thing he sees at night before going to sleep. I never thought...the uniform must have confused him."

"There's nothing to apologize for. He's excited to see his father, as I'm sure you are." Mac watched the little boy bounce on his seat, transfixed by a plane lining up on the runway, ready to make its departure.

"We haven't seen him for nine months and it's the first deployment that Christopher has been asking why his daddy was gone. Cindy here hasn't even met her daddy yet." With one hand, she tucked a pink blanket around the infant.

"My mom always said the hardest part of a deployment was when we were so young and didn't understand why our father wasn't around. It broke her heart when we were upset that he couldn't make it to our games or tuck us in, but as we grew older we began to understand. My uncle had a big role in our lives. He was military too, but their deployments didn't overlap much, so while Dad was away my uncle stepped in."

The talk of family sent his thoughts swirling down the drain to the pits. His father had missed so much of his life, just as Christopher's father was missing his children growing up, including the birth of his daughter. There was no doubt in his mind that standing up for their wonderful country was an honorable thing; he just wished there was more of a balance.

Guess that's why I never settled down or had children.

"My brother helps when he can. He lives close enough to pop over every day. It's nice to have some male influence for Christopher on a daily basis. Maybe this will be what my husband needs to get out of the service and be a proper father to his son."

The simple statement cut deeper than it should have considering he wasn't a father, but it almost implied Mac's father hadn't been a good father because he was career military. That hadn't been the case. He had been a good father, making every moment count, especially when he knew he was about to be deployed.

Military life was hard. Not everyone was cut out for it, but those who made it work were stronger than their civilian counterparts. This woman had what it took to be a military wife, but he didn't blame her one bit for wanting her man home instead of off fighting in another country. There was nothing wrong with wanting him present.

"Commander?"

He glanced back from the plane taxiing down the runway. "Please call me Mac."

"Your eyes glazed over. It was as if miles separated you from here, just as my husband does when he's thinking about a warzone. I've never understood it." She tucked a strand of her brown hair behind her ear and lowered her voice. "With all I've seen on television, I don't understand why anyone would want to let their thoughts drift back to such a place. Why can't you just let it go once you're home?"

He didn't know how to explain that the things he saw while deployed were forever burned into his brain. It wasn't something he could just turn off. The memories of the fallen warriors and the ones injured in IED explosions haunted him every time he closed his eyes. There was no shaking the ghosts he'd seen through his years in the service, but they were what kept him alive. Not one of them had died in vain.

Flashback of an ambush the year before crossed before his eyes, the same event that led to his promotion. Three of them were separated from the squad and under serious fire. Somehow, he and Bad Billy had made it out alive, determination driving them. Troy wasn't as lucky. An RPG exploded in front of him, killing him within seconds.

He squeezed the bridge of his nose and pushed the memories away. Seeing it again in his mind wouldn't change anything. The SEAL under his command had still died, and no amount of reliving it would alter the outcome.

"Ma'am, adjusting to civilian life is hard even for the best of us, but the one thing that makes it easier is having people supporting us. The memories of what we saw will never go away. Flashbacks and nightmares are something a lot of military personnel have to learn to live with once they've returned."

"Why do it then?" She looked between her children before turning back to him. "Why leave your children and family behind to go off and fight a war in another country?"

"We do it for them, to give them a better world to grow up in, and to make sure they're safe. It's better to fight the terrorists on foreign soil than here."

"I'm sorry." She shook her head, sending a curl of her brown hair falling from the clip. "It must sound like I'm complaining, but until last night when I received word that my husband was injured I never pictured my life any other way. When the officers arrived at my door…"

He laid his hand over hers. "He's going to be okay. You said it yourself."

"What about next time? Next time he might not be so lucky and my children might grow up without their father. How is that okay?" She let the tears roll down her face until they splashed off her chin. "I've seen it happen. There's no rhyme or reason why someone gets killed and another walks away. Job danger levels don't seem to matter as much as they did before, not with people shooting up our military bases. All service personnel, no matter their job—their families, even the civilians working with the military—everyone's in danger."

"It's not just military." He tried to reason with her, to allow her to see logic. "Look at our schools. How many school shootings have we had this year? Too many. Are you going to keep your kids sheltered at home, never allowing them the joys of attending school, meeting kids their own age, playing sports? Every moment of our lives there is danger lurking around the corner. We can't hibernate, scared it might be our last day. If the military has taught me one thing, it's that each day is precious and we must treat it as such. We have to live the life we were given to the fullest, not in fear."

"Now that the dangers of this war have touched my life, how am I supposed to put it behind me?"

"I don't have all the answers." He reached into his pocket for his wallet and grabbed one of the business cards he kept for cases like this. "I don't think anyone does, but she can help."

"I don't need a counselor to tell me I'm a military wife, that I have to suck it up and be supportive." She glanced down at the card but didn't take it.

"I didn't know they put it like that." He tried to joke, but it fell flat. "Honestly, Helen is the best. She knows what you're going through because she's been there. For years, she was a military spouse, fearful of that knock on her door, until one day her fear came to life, and her husband was killed in Afghanistan. She counsels spouses in your position and she can help."

The loudspeaker crackled to life, announcing their flight would be leaving soon. "Flight three seventy-five to Virginia Beach, Virginia will be boarding momentarily. Handicapped, families with children, and first class, if you will make your way to gate twenty-three we will begin."

"Ma'am, take it." He pressed the card into her hand, with the hope she'd make the call. "Over my years in the service I realized it's not just the military members sacrificing, it's also the family. You'll make it through this because you have to—and you love your husband or you wouldn't have committed to this life. He's going to need your support now more than ever."

He didn't want to pressure her to make the call, but he wanted to make sure she had the card. In the end it would be her choice. Forcing someone to seek help they didn't want did them no good, and only wasted the time of the counselor who could have been helping someone who really needed it. If anyone could help this young mother through the latest bump in the road, it would be Helen.

If she can help a worn-out, battle-hardened SEAL like me, she can help anyone.

Helen had forced him to look beyond his own guilt when he failed Troy, and look at the men who still needed him. There was no time for guilt when he had a squad counting on him to lead them. He had to pick the pieces up and get back to his duties. The cluster-fuck mission demanded he push his men harder, giving them more training. He couldn't let his guard down if they were going to survive, and he was never going to let another one of his men die.

Chapter Two

Nicole Ryan bounced one of the twins on her lap while gently rocking the baby bouncer seat with her foot. The poor sweet girls had no idea what was going on but they could feel the turmoil of the situation, and that was enough to make for a long sleepless night *again*. She had been the caregiver since the girls were born, but Shawn had always been there when she needed him, when things got harder. Now she was alone, so alone, with these two little lives depending on her at least until their guardian arrived.

Damn it, Shawn! How could you leave the girls to someone else when I've been there since the day you brought them home? I never even heard of this Mac García, and he's never even visited his grandnieces. How is he a suitable guardian?

Knowing she was going to lose these two precious girls in a matter of days broke her heart. She wouldn't even be able to see them often; they'd be across the country in Virginia. Mac would dash in and take the girls away to their new life, while she was expected to pick up the pieces and forget them. She had been there every day for six months, day and night, like a mother to the girls.

She was only the nanny. It's not as if she could really love the girls. The neighbor's rude comment at Shawn's funeral cut through her like broken glass. No one understood how she felt about the girls. How could they? *They* hadn't moved in to help after their mother had died in childbirth. There was no way Shawn could have managed twins without assistance.

If she had to blame someone for the pain she was suffering, she'd blame Shawn. He brought her into his home, let her take the place of mother to the girls, and then expected her to give them up to someone they'd never even met. She hadn't even heard of Mac until the will was read. How was he supposed to deal with twin girls when he was a bachelor and in the military?

"I'm not giving up on you girls without a fight." She pressed her lips to Gabriella's head, breathing in the baby scent mixed with the sweet lavender from the earlier bath. "You're all that's left of Shawn and he wanted so much for both of you."

With Sophia nearly asleep and Gabriella's eyes fluttering shut, she rose from the nursery rocker and stepped closer to the crib. "Come, my sweet child. Let's put you to bed." She laid the little girl in the crib, making sure to leave enough room to place Sophia next to her.

They had just begun separating the twins, forcing them into their own cribs since they were six months old and space was starting to become an issue. Since Shawn's death, they needed the comfort of being close. It had been the only way she'd been able to get them to sleep more than a short period. She had given in, seeing no other option. The girls needed each other. When things calmed down, she'd hoped to return them to their own cribs—at least she'd planned it that way until the will was read. Now it was Mac's problem.

She lifted Sophia from the bouncing seat, and the sleeping child's eyelids sprang open. "It's all right, sweetie. I'm going to put you to bed with your sister." Instead of placing her directly into the crib, she took a brief moment to snuggle the little girl tight against her chest. The children could be a handful at times but they were adorable, with their dark brown hair and sea green eyes that seemed to look directly into her soul.

With newfound determination, she swallowed the lump that had formed and laid Sophia down next to her sister. "Sleep tight, darlings. I'm going to make a call and try to keep us together." As if approving of the idea, Sophia let out a little giggle before snuggling next to Gabriella and letting her eyes close again.

Shawn, how you could have thought anyone could love these girls more than me, I'll never understand. She padded down the hall toward his office where she knew she'd find the number for Mr. Batty, the lawyer who handled Shawn's will. He would know if she had any ground to stand on when it came to retaining custody of the twins, or at the very least having visitations so she wouldn't lose contact with them.

The office still held the scent of Shawn, his crisp, fresh cologne mixing with the lingering stench of coffee. She never understood how he had managed to drink so much of it, when the smell alone churned her stomach. The large oak desk that dominated the room was where he'd spent the majority of his time when he wasn't with the girls. It was the one room she had only been in occasionally, and now that he was gone, it felt like she was invading his privacy.

Not wanting to linger, she made her way to the desk, where the leather bound planner and address book sat. She sank down on the expensive leather chair, quickly turning the pages in the book to find Mr. Batty in the address section, before her gaze moved to the papers that still cluttered his desk.

I should go through this before Mac arrives and finish getting the house ready for him, for whatever he decides to do. She had serious doubt he'd want to keep it. What use would he have for a house in a small town in Texas, when he lived in Virginia Beach? She brought the phone to her ear and dialed Mr. Batty's cell number, since it was too late to catch him in the office on a Friday.

On the second ring, he answered. "Evening, Nicole. Is everything okay?"

She couldn't keep the smile off her face. One of the best things about living in a small town was the closeness of the residents. "I need legal advice."

"I figured you'd call me when you were ready. You want to fight for the girls, don't you?"

The way he asked it, she could almost picture the older man behind his desk, surrounded by briefs, law books, and paperwork. "Do I have any grounds? I've been a part of their lives since they came home from the hospital. To hand them over to someone I didn't even know existed seems wrong with all they've been through. Shawn never even mentioned he had an uncle. Can he even take care of the girls with his career? Is it really what's best for them?"

"The law normally sides with blood relations, but they will take into consideration whatever is best for the children. In order for the uncle to maintain his career and have custody of the girls he will need to make arrangements for their care when he's on duty or deployed." She heard a glass clink against wood in the background. "All I can tell you is he'll be notified when he arrives back from the training session, and that he should be in touch with us by Monday or Tuesday. How about I come out to the house Monday morning to discuss your options? Gaining custody of the children will not give you the finances or the house. Those will still be willed to Lieutenant Commander García. You'll need to see if you have the means to raise the children on your own."

"I don't care about the money, though I admit it would be nice not to have to find a new place and shake up the girls' lives more. Still, we'd deal with it. Thank you, Mr. Batty. I'll see you on Monday."

"If it's any consolation, Shawn had the will prepared days after the girls were born. There was no one else he could have granted custody to at the time, and that will work for us. We'll see what we can do to keep the twins right here in Texas," Mr. Batty vowed before hanging up the phone.

She had a chance. That should have lifted the weight and tension, but it only made sadness join the rest of her issues. Mac might have been a good guy, one who could have been a good father to the girls…when he was home. She wouldn't deny the girls needed a father, but she couldn't give them up without a fight. She needed to at least try to give them the stable home they deserved, without more changes.

With the girls sleeping, she knew she should be doing the same. Instead, she powered on Shawn's laptop to look at the wanted ads. Before she took the job as the twins' nanny, she had been an accountant, burned out from the long hours and stressful clients. Surely she could find some accountant jobs she could do from home in between caring for the twins if she was able to get custody of them. The locals who needed accounting done could come here, or wherever she ended up living. Things were going to work out; she'd see to it. The girls were depending on her.

It was just after two in the morning when the twins' wails pulled Nicole from the first decent sleep she'd had in days, and the first dream she'd had that wasn't wrapped around Shawn's death. She slipped out of bed, grabbing her robe as she quickly made her way to the adjoining nursery. When she took the nanny position, Shawn had insisted she take the master bedroom since the nursery was closest to it, while he took another room farther down the hall by his office. It allowed her to be easily available anytime the twins needed her. Practical as it might have been, it was also sweet of him. In his own house he had taken a smaller room, and that, like so many other things, showed what a good person he was.

She'd make sure the girls knew their father was an outstanding man. He'd always been willing to drop everything at a moment's notice for someone in need, or give the shirt off his back to a friend. Shawn was an honorable man, one she grieved for every moment of the day. She grieved for herself and for the twins, who were orphans now.

She should be the one raising the girls to teach them of their father, even what little she knew about their mother. Mac knew nothing of the girls parents. How could they grow up knowing their parents loved them if they were raised by someone who didn't even know them? It sickened her, the hand life had dealt them at only six months of age. It was horrible.

"What's wrong, my beautiful girls?" She reached in and plucked out Sophia, who had most likely started the wailing, as she normally did each night. The middle of the night was when Shawn usually snuck in for a quick cuddle with the girls if they woke; it was the one time he was with them when he didn't have to worry about his cell phone ringing with some business transaction that needed his attention.

"You miss Daddy's visits, don't you?" As if in answer, Sophia's cries grew louder. "I know, my sweet girl. I miss him too. Your mommy and daddy are in Heaven watching over you." She smoothed her hand over the girl's back, trying to get her cries to subside. Gabriella had already lain back down, looking up at Nicole with her big green eyes.

"We're going to get through this," she promised, bouncing Sophia gently as the child cuddled against her chest.

She tried to convince herself that whatever happened with the custody issue, it would all work out best for them. Maybe Mac would at least allow visitation with the girls. She could be the cool aunt who popped in to visit and spoil them rotten without having to worry about being the disciplinarian. Only time would tell how things would turn out. At least she had this weekend before Mac took the girls away. *Cherish the time you have.*

Chapter Three

The late hour had the airport nearly still as Mac made his way down the terminal toward the exit. Passing the lit Christmas trees that lined the hallway, he saw embracing couples which had him speeding his pace. He needed fresh air to clear his mind and a good night's sleep to get his game back. Spending part of his journey with Shelly and her children had given him an insight he didn't have before, one that made him wonder if he had been missing something in life by not having someone to come home to. He had never planned to marry or have children of his own, not with his duties taking all of his time, but Shelly had made him wonder if he was depriving himself of something truly amazing.

Even with her unease over her husband and her questioning his career, the love was clear when she spoke about him. Hopefully, Helen would be able to help her deal with her newfound fears, but he was sure they'd make it through as long as they continued to work together and communicate. When he parted with Shelly and the children at baggage claim where her brother had met her, he could tell something had changed in her since Christopher had brought them together.

If there was one thing he knew, it was nothing ever happened without a reason. Their meeting wasn't a chance encounter; they were brought together for a purpose. Maybe something he said would help her through the trying times ahead while her husband healed. All he knew for sure was things had changed in the short time they'd spent together.

"Lieutenant Commander Mac García?"

He had been watching a family reunion and didn't notice the young Navy chaplain in his dress uniform approach him until his name was called. "Yes, Chaplain? What can I do for you?" His thoughts ran away with him as he wondered what would bring the chaplain out at such a late hour to find him. He had no family left other than his parents and brother, and he'd spoken to his father only a few hours before. Everyone was fine. That could only mean something had happened with one of his men or their families.

"Could we have a seat?" He nodded toward small seating area off to the side, and without waiting for Mac he headed to it.

"It's been a long day. If you need me to come with you on a notification, let's just go, and you can explain on the way."

The chaplain took a seat and waited for Mac to do the same. "Commander García, Thursday evening, your nephew Shawn García passed away, leaving you the custody of his twin daughters."

"Dead? Custody?" None of this could be happening. Shawn was only in his twenties, he couldn't be dead. Mac didn't even know his nephew had kids.

"The girls are six months old and their mother died in childbirth. You're the only family they have."

"Who's caring for them now?"

"A nanny, Nicole Ryan. She's been with the girls since they came home from the hospital."

It had been fifteen years since he'd seen Shawn, with only the occasional phone call shared between the two of them. Whatever possessed him to leave the children to Mac was beyond his imagination. He was a SEAL. He wasn't father material. There had to be someone more suitable. Mac liked children, but he didn't know anything about raising them. They might have been the only family Shawn and he had left, but didn't the children's mother have family who would have been more suitable to raise them?

Sink or swim, that's what the Navy taught me. Adjust and do what needs to be done.

"Commander?" The chaplain waved his hand in front of Mac's face.

"Sorry. I'm just blown away by all this. I haven't talked to Shawn in so long, I...I didn't realize his wife had...died. Jesus. She passed away in childbirth?"

"Yes."

"Poor Shawn. I apologize. What were you saying?"

"The girls are being cared for by the nanny until you arrive. Your C.O. has already cleared you of your duties while you deal with this, and there's a flight at zero six hundred hours. All you need to do is purchase a ticket and you'll have sixty days to take care of the family care plan. Is there anything else I can do for you?"

He looked at the chaplain, wanting to say *would you like a list* but he kept his mouth shut. The chaplain had to tell families their loved ones had died, and that was a duty Mac wouldn't wish on anyone. "Thank you. I better see about that ticket."

The chaplain reached into his pocket and pulled out a business card. "Here's my number if you find you need someone to confide in."

"I appreciate that, but religion has never been my scene."

"Commander, I'm more than just a religious adviser. Take the card in case." He held the card closer until Mac relented.

"I do appreciate you coming out here at this time of night to let me know." He glanced up at the clock. *After midnight.* "If it wasn't for the weather delays I would have been here earlier and I could have gotten a flight out before morning."

"The girls are in good hands until you arrive." The chaplain stood. "Safe travels."

Mac sat there long after the chaplain left, still trying to digest the news that he was now the guardian of twins. At only six months old, they would require many hours of hands-on care. How was he going to provide that? His parents were already in their sixties, so he couldn't ask for their help, and he certainly wouldn't be able to attend to them while he was on duty. How would he comply with the Family Ready Act? Retirement might be the only logical answer, and the very thought of it made him ill. What would he do with himself? Even if he retired from the military, it might be more than he could handle.

With a plane ticket to Texas in hand and hours to kill, Mac stretched out on the floor next to the window by his gate. He had slept in worse places over the years, so the dirty floor at the airport didn't bother him in the least. Something he hadn't thought about in years was eating away at him. *Religion.*

After growing up in a devoted Catholic family, he'd spread his wings at eighteen and never looked back. He believed in God, and some of the other ideas taught in church, while other things he questioned. How could a loving God send you to Hell for sex before marriage, for divorce, for suicide, and so many other so-called sins he didn't want to think about?

The way he saw it, the only people who deserved to be there were child molesters, rapists, and murderers. According to some, he was no better than a killer himself, but he didn't do it for sport or for the joy of the kill. He killed in the line of duty, for his country, when it was kill or be killed.

Over the years, he had heard plenty of hateful things about what he had done, but he refused to let any of it bother him. Now Shawn's death had brought it all to the forefront of his mind. Was he going to Hell because he chose to stand up and fight for his country, for the things he believed in? The idea of it turned his stomach. He killed to protect himself, his men, the people back home, and their way of life. To him that wasn't the same as killing in cold blood.

Maybe the old saying *two wrongs don't make a right* was correct. Killing to protect others might come with a cost, but it was one he was willing to pay. Hadn't he done his time in Hell already? Seeing what he'd seen, doing the things he had done in the name of his country. Hadn't he paid enough?

If there really was an afterlife or Heaven, he thought he should be welcomed with open arms. He'd made great sacrifices to protect the citizens of his homeland, and he'd do it again if he had to. But——

Religion.

Mac still wasn't sure how he felt about that.

A sprawling white brick ranch surrounded by trees and fields met Mac as he pulled into the driveway. Large trees thick as his waist, lent privacy to the huge property. Off to the side, he could see a pool area. The place was stunning. What had Shawn done to afford it?

Now that he was gone, Mac realized he barely knew his nephew. They hadn't spoken more than a few times a year, mostly at holidays, because there was so little left of their family. It had been almost a year since the last time they'd spoken. Mac had been deployed, and even though he'd meant to, he never got around to calling Shawn.

Now it was too late. Regret burned inside him, causing an ache to rise in his chest.

Even when they had spoken, it was quick, never more than a few minutes. No lengthy discussions about what Shawn did for a living. He knew his nephew had eloped with a local girl almost two years ago, but Mac had never met her. Over two years since his last visit. That bothered him, but there was nothing he could do to change it now.

He shoved the rental car into park in front of the house, checking one last time to make sure the address was correct before he stepped out. He glanced at the quiet house; no lights shone through the gloomy afternoon mist, leaving him to wonder if anyone was home. *I should have called ahead.* He'd taken it for granted that she'd be home with the twins.

All of a sudden, there was a grinding noise as a shotgun cocked from near the porch, sending him on guard. He stepped back next to the car, the bulk of it separating him from the front door, when a woman's voice hollered at him. "You're trespassing. This is private property."

"Ms. Ryan?" When there was no response, he continued. "Ma'am, I'm Mac García, Shawn's uncle."

"The guardian…" Her voice broke.

"Yes, ma'am. I apologize for not calling first." He watched her over the top of the car until she lowered the shotgun to the ground. Damn she was beautiful, even angry. "It's raining. May I come in?"

"Not that I have any choice. You've inherited everything and you're going to take them away from me."

He walked around the car, wondering if the plan of action he had devised through the long hours at the airport waiting for the flight had all been for nothing. The nanny might have been someone Shawn approved off, but based on first impressions he wondered if she was stable enough for the lifestyle he'd bring the children in to. *Give the woman a break. She's been through a lot.*

He stepped into the house. The large entryway with golden oak wood floors welcomed him. The outside appeared grand but inside it was warm, cozy. The smell of freshly baked bread filled the space, making it homey. It reminded him of his childhood, without the immensity of the house. Nearing forty, there were few reminders of his childhood left. Too much war, blood, and loss had separated him from those innocent years.

"Ma'am?" He glanced around in search of the woman, who had stalked off. The idea of just traipsing through the house uninvited seemed wrong, even if it was his now. To Nicole, this was her home and he respected that.

"I'm in the kitchen."

He followed her voice through the house and into a large gourmet kitchen. The white marble countertops set off the walnut cabinets, coming together in perfect elegance, while the large two-tier island was the centerpiece. He didn't doubt he'd have an easy time selling the place when he drove up, but this kitchen would have buyers fighting over the house.

"I haven't had time to prepare everything. You weren't expected until at least Monday, and the girls are asleep." She leaned against the counter, wringing her hands.

"I know. I called the lawyer on my layover to get more details since the chaplain who informed me only had the bare bones. There's an appointment with him Monday afternoon to deal with paperwork, but I had hoped to discuss things with you and possibly meet the girls."

"They're napping. If you'd have called ahead I could have kept them awake." Her tone remained cold and distant, while she stared directly at him.

"I'm sorry. Mr. Batty mentioned he'd be in touch with you. I thought you'd be expecting me." The clink of the rental car keys as they hit the counter echoed through the moment of silence. "Still, if possible, I'd like to discuss the girls with you."

"I believe anything we need to discuss can be handled through the lawyer."

"Ma'am, I understand you're grieving and that this is difficult for you…" He tried to calm the one-sided war she was trying to start, which was clear from the hatred in her voice.

"You know nothing."

"You're partially right. I know you've been with Shawn since the girls were born, but I don't know the exact relationship you had with him. Though from the hatred you're flinging at me I suspect you care deeply for the twins. This is what I want to discuss with you." He cursed inwardly; this wasn't going well.

"I have an appointment with Mr. Batty on Monday morning to file the paperwork to fight you for custody." Her hand shot up to cover her mouth as if she hadn't planned on saying that.

Feisty. I like that. He eyed the woman with new appreciation. Her shoulder length brown hair, with just the slightest wave to it, framed her face. Her brown eyes held concern and the heat of anger. She wasn't just a nanny; this woman loved the girls. So much she was willing to fight to keep them. That was devotion, just what the children needed in their lives after everything they'd already been through. Not to mention what *he* needed.

"Now that I've met you, I wouldn't expect anything less." He laid his hand over the keys and nodded. "How about I find a hotel room, shower, change, and then come back this evening? I'll meet the girls and after they're in bed for the night, we can have our discussion."

"Pinehill doesn't have a hotel. The nearest one is twenty minutes away." She tugged her hand through her hair. "Why don't you just stay here? There's plenty of room and after all, it's your house. You can get used to caring for the girls. For some reason, I suspect it will be a good learning experience for you."

"I'd appreciate it, all of it. When you're ready, we can have our talk and find some common ground went it comes to the girls. I think we can work something out without having to take this in front of a judge." At least he hoped they could, because if there was one thing he didn't want it was a custody battle. He had men depending on him and he couldn't keep his head on the missions if he was fighting a lengthy court battle. They'd have to find a way to work together, keeping what was theirs safe and happy. Together—that was the only way.

Chapter Four

With a basket of freshly washed baby clothes in her arms, Nicole collapsed on the sofa in the family room. Between the girls' unease, and her own grief, she was exhausted. Sleep had once been easy, now it was a fight for even the smallest amounts. Normally after a rough night with the girls, she'd take a nap to help prepare for the wakeup calls in the night, but sleep wasn't an option with Mac in the house.

She had prepared herself to hate him for his part in separating her from the girls, but now that he was here, it was proving more difficult then she imagined. Damn, the way he looked in the Navy working uniform, with its standard camouflage of blue and gray, stole her breath. He was an attractive man, the slightest hint of silver around his temples adding a pleasant imperfection she couldn't help but find alluring.

She had to keep her distance from him, build a barrier between them in order to keep him from ripping her heart out when he whisked the girls away—and tearing the rest of her to shreds in the process. The last six months had changed her, more than just turning her into a stand-in mother. She'd realized her calling, and it was with the girls.

Being burned out with accounting was a blessing, because it had brought her this makeshift family for a short time.

Piece by piece she folded the laundry, and with each article of clothing she tried to form the walls around her before Mac returned. She needed a game plan, something that would give her the advantage when she faced him with her desire to keep the children, to raise them as her own. If she went at him with the rage that burned within her, it would get them nowhere. She had to prove she was a better option for them than he was, otherwise they'd be off to Virginia before she even got a court date. Every ounce of her knew that if they left Texas, she'd never see the girls again.

She heard a small cough, and looked up from stacking the freshly folded laundry in the basket to find Mac standing near the doorway. Stonewashed jeans slung low on his hips, encasing his legs to show hints of the toned thigh muscles beneath the denim. The gray T-shirt with bright blue *Navy* across the chest had her fingers itching to run along the contours of his body. She thought he looked good in uniform, but in plain clothes he looked even better. She bet he was irresistible naked. Every muscle in his body was toned to rock-hard perfection and his tanned skin highlighted each feature. Overall, he was one fine specimen of manhood. *Not to mention he probably had a woman at every port.*

"Mind if I join you?"

"Please." She nodded to the recliner beside her. "If I'm lucky, the girls will sleep for another hour, so you can rest if you want. I mean, from what Mr. Batty said, you were on your way back from military duty, so you must have come straight here after you arrived. I'm sure you're exhausted."

"My squad was out for training. They returned Thursday, while I stayed behind to deal with a few things. I got to Virginia after midnight and the chaplain was waiting with the news, so I caught the first flight here." He slumped down onto the chair beside her. "I caught a bit of sleep on the plane…but suddenly I have a feeling you're using this as a diversion. I don't think it worries you that I'm tired."

"Diversion, why?" She put the basket on the coffee table and moved to the edge of the sofa.

"I wanted to speak with you about the girls and coming to an arrangement. When I mentioned it, you informed me that you intend to seek custody."

"I do." She pushed off the sofa and grabbed the basket. "I don't believe there's anything for us to discuss."

"Well, I do, so sit down and we can deal with it before the girls wake up."

"I'm not one of your men you can just order around," she snapped, tossing the basket down with such force a couple of the garments on top bounced, unfolding them slightly. *Work with him or you'll never see the girls again.* "I'm sorry for being such a bitch. It's been a whirlwind few days…"

"Ma'am I realize you're under a great amount of stress. From what Mr. Batty told me you've been the girls' nanny since Shawn brought them home from the hospital."

"Stop with this ma'am crap, you make me feel old with it. The name's Nicole, and I've been more than a nanny to Gabriella and Sophia. They are like my own children." Her throat grew tight and tears threatened to fall.

The anger burning within her just wanted an outlet. Mac was a victim to circumstances, just as she was. Maybe he didn't want the children after all and he had come to Texas to give up his rights. Maybe there was no need for a court battle.

Cries from the baby monitor stopped her from screaming at him for coming to take her little ones away. "I've got to take care of the girls." She pivoted on her heels and headed toward their room before he could reply. The perfect break from the madness that had become her life.

Nicole paced the nursery with a fussy Gabriella in her arms, while Mac held Sophia in the rocker. For the first time since he arrived, she was thankful for his help. Having two sick babies at the same time alone was almost more than anyone could handle. The mixture of the wails from both of the twins only served to make her nervous. Nothing they tried eased the girls' discomfort, and Doctor Holt wasn't answering his phone, not even his cell. She left messages everywhere she could think of, asking him to call her, but he was probably traveling to or from the hospital, in an area that had almost no cell coverage. She looked at the clock for the hundredth time.

Doctor Holt, I need you.

The girls wouldn't eat or sleep and nothing seemed to ease their cries. Her nerves were frazzled. The worst part of motherhood was when a child was hurting and there was nothing that could be done to ease the pain.

"Oh, darling, if I knew what would make you feel better, I'd do it." She rubbed small circles up and down her back.

"Isn't there something we should be doing?" Mac nearly hollered at her over the cries. "Take them to the doctor, hospital, or something?"

"Doctor Holt is the only doctor in Pinehill and he isn't answering his cell phone."

Mac stood, lifting Sophia higher up his chest, until her head rested against his shoulder. She looked so small in his arms.

Mmm, those arms. Even in the midst of the twins' cries, her body reacted to the man standing before her. Something about him with Sophia in his arms made him that much more attractive. *Settle down, girl, he's out of your league.*

"Where the fuck is Rebel when I need him?"

"Rebel?" She focused on that so she'd ignore his language. She understood he was in the military, and foul language was often part of the territory, but she didn't want it around the girls. She didn't want their first words to be a curse word.

"Luke Rodríguez, everyone calls him Rebel, he's my team's medic and can patch up just about anything. Me, on the other hand…I'm hopeless when it comes to these sick girls. Maybe we should take them to the hospital."

"I had hoped Doctor Holt would call, but we can't wait any longer. We have to do something." She laid Gabriella back in the crib, and that only made her cries louder. "It's okay, sweetie, I just need to get the diaper bag ready."

"Give her to me. I'll hold her while you get the stuff together." He held out his free arm.

"Are you sure?" It was the logical solution, but he'd just admitted this was his first experience with young children. Even with that in mind, he had a natural way with them; the more comfortable he got with the girls, the more it showed.

"It's fine, unless you need me to do something."

"No, just hold them while I gather what we need. We'll have to take Shawn's SUV, since it has the car seats." She lifted Gabriella from the crib and kissed the girl's head. The heat from her forehead made Nicole sick with worry. "Five minutes, that's all I need."

With the hospital's address plugged into the GPS, Mac pushed the petal to the floorboard until the outside rushed by with such speed it was nauseating. He glanced in the rearview mirror at the girls. They were still crying but the car had soothed them a little. Nicole adjusted in the passenger seat and drew his attention. The terror in her eyes made him want to console her, but he wouldn't give her false hope. He knew next to nothing about children, but his gut told him the crying wasn't normal. He didn't like to see them suffering; it tore at his stomach like nothing he'd ever experienced. When it was one of his men, they knew why and what to do to fix it. With the girls, he couldn't do anything and they couldn't tell him what was wrong.

"We'll be there in a few minutes."

"Not soon enough." Her voice was raspy with unshed tears. "I've never seen them like this before. Not even when they had colic after they were born."

In answer to her comment, he pushed the car a little harder. "We'll handle it."

Fifteen minutes later, he stood at the desk in the emergency room doing his best to fill out the registration forms, while Nicole stood behind him trying to soothe the twins, who were wailing louder and louder.

"I thought I heard a familiar cry." Doctor Holt closed one of the exam room doors and came to stand by them. "What seems to be the problem with the happy–go–lucky García girls?"

"Doc, I'm so glad you're here. They've been sick all day. Their crying won't stop as if they're in pain, and it's been getting worse, not better. Nothing I've done has helped. Neither of them will eat or sleep."

"Come along. We'll take a look at them." The doctor turned and hit the button on the wall. The doors slid open.

Not sure what else to do, Mac followed helplessly with the diaper bag and clipboard from the check-in desk. Never in all his life had he felt like this. He was a man of action; give him a problem, and he would find a way to fix it. Give him a mission, and consider it done. This was something he couldn't fix, and it got under his skin.

Taken straight to one of the patient rooms, Nicole lifted Sophia from the stroller and laid her on the bed. Mac stepped around the doctor to pick Gabriella up and try to give her some comfort. He stayed near the edge of the bed, out of the way, while the doctor did his work. Feeling like an outsider, his gaze shifted between Nicole who cringed with every tearful wail and Sophia who tried to wiggle away from the doctor's cold stethoscope.

Hours before, he'd shown up at the door, hoping to convince her they could figure out a way to work together to raise the twins. Now he knew there was no other way. No matter the cost, they had to figure it out. The girls needed her in their lives, and she needed them. They were a family, something he envied because he wasn't included—*yet*.

Doctor Holt examined both of the girls, checking their temperature before listening to their chests intently. "We'll need to run some tests. In the meantime, I'll give them something to help with the hives and make them more comfortable."

"What's wrong with them?" Tears shimmered in her eyes, threatening to fall.

"I want to do blood work to confirm, but it looks like allergies. Have you introduced any new foods?"

She nodded, looking down at the girls. "Oatmeal."

"That's what I thought. They're both dehydrated, so we'll start an IV with fluids. With their age and the extent of their reaction, I want to rule out anything more dangerous, but I believe with some medication, they'll be fine. They've worked themselves up by crying so much. The nurse will be in shortly to give them something, and I'll be back once the results are in. If you need anything let the nurse know."

As Doctor Holt left, Mac watched Nicole's strength dissipate, and her knees buckled. He reached out, hooking his arm around her waist, and kept her from collapsing into a heap on the floor. "Come sit down." He directed her to the hardback chair next to the bed.

"Allergies," she whispered, her voice cracking. "I should have thought about that. I could have killed them."

"Nicole, this isn't your fault. How were you supposed to know?"

"I've been a mother to these girls since they were born and I've let them down."

"A lot of people have allergic relations to something. Don't go borrowing trouble. They're going to be fine." He ran his hand up and down her arm. "Everything is going to be fine."

"How is this going to look to a judge?" She reached down, letting Sophia's fingers tighten around her forefinger.

"I hope it won't get to that. As I tried to tell you before, I think I have an option that will work for us..."

"Ms. Ryan." The nurse entered the room, interrupting him before he could continue. "I'm here to set up the IV and draw blood. The medication the doctor ordered should be brought up by the time I'm finished."

Nicole looked from the girls to the nurse and finally nodded. "Do you want me to hold them while you start the IV? They're not going to stay still. They won't quit crying, I've tried everything." The girls breathed raggedly from the state they'd worked themselves into.

"Why don't you take a break? Get some coffee or something," the nurse suggested while preparing the IV rack.

"No." Nicole's answer was harsh, as if she couldn't believe the nerve of the nurse. "I'm staying with them."

"Ma'am, do whatever you need to, but we're staying." He ran his hand along Gabriella's back in soothing circles.

The nurse nodded before going about her business, prepping the IV. While she attended to the IVs, Mac took a moment to watch Nicole and how she was with the girls. There was a bond between them, stronger than he had believed was possible. She loved them as her own, and they loved her.

Why had Shawn left him the girls when it was clear she should have custody? He might have thought money was the issue if he hadn't already been told the inheritance figures, not to mention the house could be sold if needed which in itself would be a nice sum. Whatever the reason, he needed to see if he could figure it out before they took the next step.

"Mary, here's the medication." Another nurse stepped into the room and pulled him from his thoughts.

"Good. These little girls have worked themselves into such a state, not to mention their poor mamma." She grabbed the syringe from the other woman. "This should only take a few minutes to work. It'll probably put them to sleep, which is what they need." Taking a firm hold of Sophia's chubby arm, she wiped the area with an alcohol cloth before she eased the needle home with the expertise acquired from years of experience.

Mac wasn't sure it was possible, but their cries grew louder after the injection until he was sure everyone in the hospital heard them. His chest tightened as the sound cut through him. He'd rather hear gunfire, RPGs, or his men; the pitiful cries of these girls left him useless. At least in battle he could do something, not stand around. His first day as the girls' guardian, and they were already in the hospital. This didn't give him much hope for the future.

"They should calm shortly," the nurse said before slipping out the door.

The IV slowly replenished the girls, while Nicole and he both took one of the twins. During their best to soothe them, they rubbed along their backs, wiping away their tears, giving them gentle caresses. Eventually, the sobs turned into soft whimpers and the girls cuddled together on the hospital bed, their eyes fluttering as the medication began to pull them into a deep sleep.

With the tears gone, his sleep deprivation began to creep up on him. He leaned against the wall, wondering where Doctor Holt was with the test results. "They're going to be fine."

She sat there staring at the almost asleep girls with tears in her eyes, and smoothed the hair away from Sophia's face.

"Nicole, look at me." He took his forefinger and softly turned her head toward him. "You okay?" He had seen shock in his men before but this was something different. It was almost like she was grieving. Her shoulders slouched into her, and her eyes glazed with distance.

"I was just thinking…" Tears fell freely down her cheek. "I don't know what I would do without them. Six months doesn't seem like that long, but my life has revolved around them day in and day out. I love them as if they were my own flesh and blood, maybe more because I chose them."

"We'll work something out." In that moment, he knew the girls needed someone like her in their life. It wasn't just the fact he needed someone to care for them when he was on military duty, because he could always make other arrangements, but this was about keeping a family together. It might not have been a blood family, but it was still a family in its own right.

Chapter Five

Nicole swirled the last remaining coffee in the bottom of the cup Mac had brought her twenty minutes ago while they waited for the IV to finish its cycle. It had been a long night for everyone involved, but for her it had been a long few days. Part of her wanted to fast-forward a few months in the future to find out what would happen with the custody of the girls, while the other part wanted to cherish every moment she had with them.

There was no balance to her wants, but the grief of losing them was already manifesting within her and grew stronger when she thought about the first impression she'd given Mac of her parenting skills. She beat herself up for not catching the allergic reaction sooner, but when it came down to it, it would look bad in court no matter what.

Maybe I shouldn't even go forward with the custody dispute. I'll lose anyway. Cut my losses now, grieve, and maybe he'll allow me visitation. If I fight him in court and lose, I'll never see the girls again.

Out of the corner of her eye, she caught Mac jerk as he came awake in a flash. She knew he was exhausted and had tried to get him to go back to the house to sleep since all they were doing was waiting for the IV to finish, but he wouldn't leave. She guessed he was trying to prove he could be a good guardian, just as she was, and if he left it wouldn't look well for him in court either. Now she understood why people said every little thing could work or hurt them in a custody battle.

"You okay?"

"Yeah, fine." He ran a hand over his face and set up straight. "Sorry, I guess I fell asleep."

She was going to tell him to go back to the house for the umpteenth time but Doctor Holt and the nurse who started the IV walked in before she could say a word.

"Mary tells me the García twins are doing much better. Allergic reactions are subsiding." He took his stethoscope from around his neck and listened to each of the girls' chests, neither of them waking. "I'm going to write you a prescription for any future allergic reactions. We can run allergy tests but my guess would be the wheat in the oatmeal caused the reaction."

"Twins can have the same allergy?"

"Identical twins only have an approximate sixty percent chance that they will share the allergy, but I think it's clear Gabriella and Sophia share it," Doctor Holt explained. "As long as you avoid wheat there should be no future reactions."

"Thank you, Doctor Holt." She rose from the chair to stand by the bed while the nurse removed the IVs.

"I'll see them for their regular checkup the beginning of the month." Doctor Holt turned to leave.

"Actually…" She glanced toward Mac. "I believe you'll be receiving a request for their files. This is Lieutenant Commander Mac Garcia; he's Shawn's uncle and the children's new guardian."

"Lieutenant Commander, that's Navy right? I was in the Army."

Mac rose and held out his hand to the doctor. "Yes sir. I'm a SEAL."

SEAL, isn't that one of the most prestigious and difficult positions? She wracked her brain trying to remember what she knew about Navy SEALs, but it was very little. How was he going to care for the girls with that type of career? Would he give it up to be a father? She doubted that; everything about him screamed career military. Her stomach turned, thinking that if he took the girls away from her, they could end up with another death. He could die in action and the girls would be left alone—*again.*

Blow after blow for her precious twins. How much could they take? How much could she stand by and let happen? It was all becoming too much for her. At least the girls were too young to understand the situation.

Darkness had settled over the sleepy town of Pinehill by the time they made it back to the house and got the girls into their crib. Exhaustion filled every muscle in Nicole's body as she plopped down on the sofa. She didn't have the strength to get up and go to bed, plus she had hoped for a moment with Mac before they both collapsed for the night. She didn't have the energy to fight about custody tonight, she only had one question. One that couldn't or wouldn't wait until they woke.

"I'm going to hit the sack but if the girls wake and you need some help please just holler. I should hear them, but if my exhaustion knocks me out, please come get me." He stood in the kitchen entry with a glass of water in hand. "Unless you want me to stay in your room and you can take the night off."

"Absolutely not!"

"I just thought…" He shook his head. "You're right, you know where I am if you need me."

"Wait." She forced herself to scoot up the sofa, to look him in the eye. "You're a SEAL."

"Yes ma'am." He raised an eyebrow in question as if he wondered why she was asking. "I enlisted in the Navy when I was eighteen, over twenty years ago."

"I admit I wasn't paying attention when you spoke with Doctor Holt, but I got the impression that Lieutenant Commander was an officer."

"It is. The Navy was my ticket to college. I received my degree in engineering, went to officer school, and was commissioned as an officer some time ago. What is this about?"

"Mr. Batty told me you were military, but I didn't realize you were a SEAL. I pulled it up on my phone while you were talking to Doctor Holt. It's dangerous." Her chest tightened with the thought of him risking himself in the way he did.

"Not if you do it right." He smirked and sat the glass of water on the end table. "It's been a long day, we're both tired. Why don't you just tell me why my job bothers you?"

"I'm worried about the girls. If I lose the custody battle, I want to know they're safe and in a good home. That wouldn't be the case with your job. Are you willing to retire from the Navy to care for the children?"

"This is something I've tried to discuss with you but we've been interrupted. I had planned to try again after we both got some sleep, but we can do it now." He came to sit on the opposite end of the sofa, his back against the armrest so he could watch her. "With twenty years in, I'm able to retire and be fine, but it's not something I want. I've given this some thought since I spoke with the chaplain. I want to continue my career, because I love what I do and I'm good at it. I don't know how to be a civilian."

"What about the girls? Where do they fit in with your *career*?"

"In the military, single parents must have a family care plan. Basically, it requires me to have a nonmilitary person to care for the girls while I'm on duty. Since I'm a SEAL this means they would be on call at all times, every day and all year, because I could be called for a mission at any time. After giving this some thought I've come up with something that I believe would work for both of us. I'd like you to come back to Virginia with me, to care for the children."

"What?" She couldn't believe what she was hearing.

"I'll continue whatever payment Shawn had with you, or we could work something else out."

"This isn't about the money. You want me to just pick up and move, to disrupt the girls even further when you're not even going to be a parent to them like they need? Instead, you're going to put your career before them and expect me to be *both* parents. At least Shawn was a part of their lives."

Anger sparked to life, burning low in her gut. She wanted to let the anger strike out, to scream about the nerve he had. Did he honestly think picking up the girls, moving them to Virginia, and inserting himself into their life would be easy? If so, he had a rude awakening coming. The girls' lives were already turned upside down and it was displayed in their behaviors.

"I'll admit my job takes me away often, either on training or missions, but it doesn't mean I can't be a parent. There are a lot of military families out there with young children. I'm aware the girls are going to have a difficult time adjusting, but I think with you there for them, things will be easier."

"No." She forced herself beyond the exhaustion and onto her feet. "How dare you? Don't expect me to just pick up and move to Virginia to be both parents to them. If I'm doing that, I'll do it here."

"I'm not talking about a custody battle. I'm offering us both an alternative, one that will give the girls both of us. The way you look at them proves you love them, and I'm the last blood relative they have. Is there anyone better to help raise them than us? I understand what I'm asking if difficult, it means moving across the country and starting over, possibly with me away a good portion of the time…but isn't giving the girls a family with both of us the most important thing?"

"Mac…" She stared down at him, completely baffled, but before she could say anything more he stopped her.

"Before you say no, I only ask that you think about it. We've had a long night, and should sleep while the girls are. Just think about it and we can talk about it in the morning. If you're unwilling maybe we could come to another arrangement." He stood from the sofa. "Just consider it."

He left her standing there, utterly bewildered. Move to Virginia Beach and raise the girls while he was off in some foreign land fighting a war that seemed like it would never end? What if he was killed, what would happen to the girls then? No, she needed to fight him for custody now, because if he died on a mission, she'd have no right to the children anymore. Even though they might not remember it, they didn't need to lose another person.

Knowing that sleep was out of the question until she calmed the turmoil raging within her, she made her way to Shawn's office. There she could make herself useful, organizing things that still needed to be dealt with, and hopefully making it a little simpler for Mac.

That selfish bastard, why do I even care? I should just wash my hands of everything and leave him to deal with it. But it wasn't like her to do something like that. Instead, she'd do what she could to make things easier for him—but most importantly for the girls.

They were the ones who would suffer if he won custody and took them to Virginia. Forcing a new caregiver onto them wouldn't be easy and would make the adjustment that much harder.

Maybe I should take him up on his offer. If I lose the custody battle, the offer won't stand and will only hurt the girls more. She was in a difficult spot, because both options risked something—the children or her. Moving to Virginia would be an easy solution, but being with him on a near daily basis, and caring for the girls while he was their guardian, would prove to be a challenge and potentially disastrous to her soul. Not to mention her heart.

She stepped into Shawn's office, the familiar spiciness of his cologne engulfing her, sending a pain of longing through her. Over the past six months, she and Shawn had bonded quickly, becoming best friends. Now she wasn't sure how to deal, especially when she was about to lose the last remaining parts of him—the twins.

Every day without him made the ache in her heart grow more painful. At first, she wasn't sure how she'd get through the minutes without him, but somehow she did. Minutes became days and eventually days would become months and even years. She pulled herself together enough to carry on for the sake of the children. If Mac took them away from her, would she be able to carry on with her life?

There amongst the computer print-offs, a piece of Shawn's thick personal stationary laid almost buried, only a few strokes of his messy handwriting peeking out to draw her attention. She wondered why she hadn't seen it until now. She sank down on the chair and pulled it free. The date at the top of the stationary was the day before he died.

Just as I could feel something was off the night the girls were born, I know something is wrong now. Only this time it won't be my wife, it will be me. I can't explain how I know this, but my time is coming to an end, and I will leave my girls as orphans. Just knowing this is heartbreaking…my girls, my sweet Gabriella and Sophia.

Nicole, if you're reading this, I know you're wondering why I wouldn't fight it, so know this—if I can, I will. I have already been to Doctor Holts for a complete checkup. I told him I just wanted to make sure I was in perfect health now that I was a single parent. He found nothing wrong. Maybe it won't be a health issue that ends my life, but that's the only one I know I can fight. What else am I supposed to do? Lock myself in the house?

I have secured a future for them without financial worries and on Monday I'll contact Mr. Batty to add Nicole to my will. I don't know how they'll do it, but Nicole…you and Mac will have to raise the girls. You're probably wondering why I wouldn't grant just one of them custody. That's because the girls need both of them. They need a family. If anyone can bond together to raise them as I would have, it's them. Uncle Mac is a good man but with his career, he couldn't raise them on his own. They need a mother. Not a mother, their mother—Nicole—she might not be their biological mother but she has given them the love, nurturing, and everything my beautiful wife would have. I know with Nicole they will never lack in the love department, and Mac can be the father I can't be.

When Gabriella and Sophia are old enough to understand, I hope they will be told of us, in the meantime I would like if Nicole and Mac raised them as their own. Give them the true family I won't be able to give them. Don't misread this. I don't expect them to have a relationship together. Uncle Mac is far too dedicated to his career for any relationship—but they can become friends just as Nicole and I have, and raise my sweet Gabriella and Sophia together. One day I hope that Nicole will find a man who will make her happy. She will marry and have children of her own, because she's an amazing mother to the twins. They'll work out something then, to keep both Mac and Nicole in the girls' lives.

If I have to leave my girls, I know I couldn't leave them in better hands than Nicole and Uncle Mac. They will protect my beautiful girls from everything and everyone. Mac will be the father I would have been when the girls start to date, scaring away the boys until the perfect ones come along. While Nicole will be there to soothe the bumps and bruises along the way, to mend their hearts, have late night chats, and bake her delicious cookies.

My sweet Gabriella and Sophia, I love you, and I have no doubt you will be in good hands.

Nicole, take good care of my babies. Make sure they know their parents loved them, and most of all know I'll always be with you. You're amazing and I couldn't have asked for a better woman to come into our lives after my wife died. You gave me the strength to carry on, and for that I'll always be grateful. Thank you.

With tears streaming down her face, she set the letter aside. This letter was enough to at least gain partial custody of the girls, but knowing what Shawn had wanted changed things. How could she fight Mac when Shawn wanted them to work together? She knew she should value his last wishes, and move to Virginia. But it didn't make it easier.

I don't know how I supposed to raise the girls with a man I barely know—a man who sends my heart racing.

All she could do was try. Give it her best shot, and make Shawn proud.

Chapter Six

Mac woke before the sun peeked over the horizon, his thoughts instantly returning to the last conversation he'd had with Nicole before he crashed. He wanted to do it gently, to ease her into the idea of returning to Virginia with him. Instead, he'd blurted it out like an idiot. He hadn't been this uneasy and unsure of himself since his first year as an officer; leading his men for the first time had been almost as bad.

His men, the damn squad of SEALs, was becoming family central. First Ace and Gwen, with their beautiful daughter Roulette. Now Boom and Wynn were expecting their first child in June. The once squad of eight single men dedicated to the SEALs were now starting families of their own. Eventually some of them would move on, leaving the SEALs behind for a safer career, one that would keep them home. This was the first hint that one day the eight men he'd been leading since he was commissioned as an officer would someday be divided. With each blink of an eye, the world changes, sometimes for the good and other times for the bad, and only time would tell which direction things went.

He scooted up in bed, pressing his back against the headboard. The need for coffee hit him but he worried that if he got up and started moving about in the kitchen he'd wake Nicole. After the night they had, she deserved to be able to sleep in if the girls didn't wake her first.

There was something about that woman that drove him wild. He hadn't been drawn to another woman as he was with her in years. There had been occasional women in his life, but none of them had lasted longer than a few weeks. His career was too demanding for most women to be willing to put up with it, let alone think long-term. Why should he suspect it would be any different with Nicole? Because he proposed they raise the twins together in Virginia? If anything, that would make her more likely to run. What did he have to offer her? Nothing compared to what she was living in now.

His house was comfortable, but didn't offer the luxury of Shawn's home, especially since he was in the middle of remodeling it. There were no marble floors, no swimming pool half the size of a football field. His place held the same privacy with over six acres, and trees adding to the secluded atmosphere. He'd purchased it three years ago for a good price because of its run-down state. Now when he wasn't on military duty he was restoring the French colonial. There were still things he'd need to get done before the girls were walking, including baby-proofing the house.

Baby-proofing the house, look how far I've fallen. He couldn't believe he was thinking about child proofing his house. A man who couldn't even keep a woman long-term and somehow he was supposed to raise twin girls. What did he know about females, or even raising children?

A tap came from the door, so light he thought he wasn't sure he even heard it. "Come in?" He almost thought his ears were playing a trick on him.

The door he had left open a crack swung open. "Mac?"

"Come in. Is it the girls?" He reached for the shirt he'd draped over the bedpost before he fell asleep.

"No, the girls are still asleep. I couldn't sleep and thought you might be awake. Could we talk?" She stood in the doorway, her hand on the doorknob.

"Sure. Come sit, or we can go to the kitchen."

"It will only take a minute, then you can go back to sleep, or whatever you want to do." She stepped closer to the edge of the bed, her gaze darting from his chest to anywhere else.

"*Merda.*" He grabbed his shirt and tugged it over his head. It had been too long since a woman had seen him without his shirt; he had forgotten his scars tended to make people uncomfortable. They always reminded them just how dangerous his job was. "Sorry."

"It's my fault, and not for the reason you think." She shook her head. "I want to discuss me coming to Virginia to help raise the girls, but first I think you should read this." She held out a piece of stationary.

"What is it?"

"It's Shawn's last letter, written the day before his death. He knew...read it. I'll get us coffee and be right back." She didn't wait for him to reply, instead she scurried out the door.

Bringing it close enough to read, he recognized his nephew's handwriting from the occasional letters they'd exchanged over the years. How did Shawn know he'd die? Would he have changed the will? His mind overflowed with questions he didn't have the answers to. He was already invested in the girls. What if this letter said he wanted Nicole to have custody of them? Could he just walk away from them?

Nicole couldn't get the image of Mac's chest out of her mind. She wanted to go to him, rub her hand over the contours of his chest, explore the taut muscles under her fingertips, the puckered and indented skin around each scar. What had he experienced to cause them? Suffering the actions of war, seeing the things he had seen, how could he still be sane? She had heard of some of the troops coming back with post-traumatic stress disorder, suffering from nightmares. Some of them never returned to normal. Did Mac have any issues she needed to be concerned with?

Her mind jumped from one thing to another. Was he like some of the other military men she met with woman all over the world? Did she need to worry there might be a different woman every week, or every month, in the girls' lives? How would she explain that to them as they got older? As the questions raced through her mind, she realized she had already agreed to go to Virginia with him, in order to keep the girls. She just hoped he would meet a few of her requests.

"Knowing Shawn wanted us to raise the girls together, are you still going to fight for custody?" Mac startled her, nearly making her drop the pot of coffee.

She sat the pot back in the coffeemaker, turned to him, and held out a mug. "I'll go to Virginia with one request."

"Name it."

"We sign the custody papers for the girls together. Give me the same rights to them as you have—joint custody. It will help if you're deployed and they need medical care, to be enrolled in school as they get older, but most importantly because it's what Shawn wanted...and what I want. To me, those girls are my daughters."

"Compromise." He sat the coffee aside and watched her. "Come spend Christmas with me in Virginia. If everything goes okay, we'll sign the papers for joint custody. If things don't go as planned, we can work something else out. It's going to take time for the official paperwork to be drawn up anyway, and it's only two weeks until Christmas. In the meantime I won't sell the house, or deal with any of that in case you wish to return."

"It's not my house, it's yours."

"If you wish to return and take the girls, at least I would know you have a good home. One that will keep you and the girls protected and where they can be raised without moving around from place to place. If we need to, we'll split the time with the girls, though I'm sure Shawn would want us to raise them together on a daily basis, and I'll admit it's what I want too." He came to stand in front of her, his hand laying over hers on the counter. "When I was a young boy my best friend's father died, and it's something I could never forget. His father was military, but he was killed in a motorcycle accident, and the police showed up on a dark rainy night while I was spending the night with him, to tell his mother what happened. After that, the family moved around, apartment to apartment, his mother taking whatever waitressing jobs she could find until she needed to move on. I remember what they suffered, how my best friend was never the same. I want the girls to grow up in a home, not just a house but a real home, that no matter how old they are they can always come back to."

"That sounds nice." Many times, she wished she had that very thing. "Giving the girls a home is very important to me. If we can bond as Shawn and I did to raise the girls together, that would be even better. They deserve a proper family, at least as much as we can give them."

"So you agree, you'll come spend the holidays with me and then we can tackle the legal paperwork?"

"Okay, but I want to give them a proper Christmas, with trees, decorations, and all the festive stuff. It's their first Christmas, and though I don't feel like celebrating I want to make it special for Gabriella and Sophia. They won't remember it, but we'll have the pictures."

"We'll make it the best Christmas for all of us. We deserve it."

The idea of spending Christmas with him sent her heart racing. It seemed more intimate than it should have been. They were supposed to develop a friendship, nothing more. But if that was true, why did his body call to her like a candle to a flame?

My SEAL. She didn't have a right to think like that. Not to mention that getting involved with him could be disastrous. If things went wrong it could have dramatic effects on her relationship with the girls. No, for their sake she had to keep things purely platonic with Mac. Now if she could only convince her erotic thoughts of that fact.

He gave her hand a gentle squeeze. "Anything you want just let me know, and I'll do my best to see it happen. After all, this is a new start for all of us."

A new start...she tried not to read further into it, but her stomach fluttered with the possibilities. "When do we leave?"

"We both have appointments with Mr. Batty tomorrow, so how about the next day? It will give us time to get settled and ready for Christmas." He paused and took a long drink of the coffee.

"I can pack most of what the girls need, but we'll still need at least one crib."

"Boom's wife Wynn—he's one of my men—is about to launch a new store, Heart of Diamond, which mostly carries her own designs for baby and toddler outfits. I'll call her and see if we can arrange for it to be at the house when we arrive. Anything else we can purchase once we're there."

"As long as we have a crib, we can make do. Traveling with them isn't going to be easy." She chuckled at the thought. *Easy* was an understatement. She and Shawn had tried to take the girls to California for a business trip when they were three months old and he didn't want to leave them. Three hours away, and they turned the SUV around, and threw in the towel. They were fine on short trips but got fussy the longer it went.

Shawn, I miss you so much.

She closed her eyes, trying to keep the tears that threatened to fall hidden, but they escaped and splashed down her face. Would there ever be a time when the memories of Shawn didn't tear her heart to shreds? She tried to breathe, to force the air into her tightening chest, and the memories of him away. Mac's brushed his thumb against her cheek, wiping away the tears that had fallen.

"I didn't mean to upset you."

"It wasn't you." She opened her eyes to look at him, only to see the same pain she felt. She wondered why he was upset; he barely knew Shawn. "I can't think of Shawn without regret and deep loss."

"Regret? Shawn died in a car accident. What is there to regret?"

"My grandmother…" Her voice cracked before she could gain control of her emotions. "I spent so much time with her, especially after the problems with my dad. Almost two years ago, she passed away without a will. Because of the medical bills, her cottage was claimed by the collectors and was being sold. On the day he died, Shawn was out because of the auction. He was going to purchase it. If I hadn't told him I wanted that damn cottage, he'd have been home with the girls like he should have been."

"That's not your fault." He wrapped his arm around her shoulders. "We can talk about the *ifs* all day long, but it doesn't change things. I learned long ago that when it's our time, nothing can stop death."

"You've seen the worst, haven't you? Men dying."

He winced at her comment and sadness filled his forest green eyes as his look became distant. "More than I care to remember."

Wanting to ease the pain she saw in his eyes, she wrapped her arms around him. He was such a strong man, one who believed in fighting for their country, even after all the death and injuries he'd seen. He'd fight through the worst to keep America safe, and she admired that. She only prayed he wouldn't become another casualty, not while she and the girls needed him.

Standing there with her arms around his waist, his cologne drifting past her nose, she could feel herself drawn to him and needed to know if there was someone else before she let things got too far. She hadn't felt a connection to anyone like this since her college boyfriend, who ended up taking a job in California and leaving her behind to start her accounting business. But she needed something with more freedom, with children. That's when she saw Shawn's ad and she never looked back. Everything happened for a reason, but if Mac had someone in his life, she needed to stop this before it could go any further.

"May I ask something personal?"

"Go ahead." There was a slight hesitation in his voice.

"I don't see a wedding ring on your finger, but is there someone in your life? A fiancée? Girlfriend? Anyone I should worry about who might have issues with this?"

"With this?" Smirking, he raised an eyebrow at her.

"I meant the arrangement of us raising the girls together. If there's someone else—" She wasn't sure where she was going with that, but thankfully he cut her off before she could finish.

"There's no woman in my life, just my career, and the house. If I'm not on duty, I'm working on the house. It's an old French colonial, with over six acres. When I purchased it three years ago it was pretty run-down, so I've been restoring it." He slipped his hand up from the small of her back. "Why do you ask, beautiful, are you interested?"

"I…" She stammered, hating she was that obvious, before she pulled herself together. "I was asking for the girls' sake. They're going to have a hard enough time adjusting, so the less interruptions they have the better. Adding new people right now isn't going to make things easier."

"Whatever you say." He smirked, almost as if he didn't believe her.

Nice one, Nicole. She'd just met him and she was already coming across as some cheap slut. The fact that he was drop-dead sexy wasn't enough for a relationship, and she didn't know anything about him. All the time they'd spent together had been because of the twins, anything they talked about was regarding them. Hell, she had threatened to take him to court for custody; that wasn't the best way to start any kind of relationship, let alone a romantic one.

She wasn't sure getting involved with him was a good thing; it risked too much when it came to the twins. If things went badly, it was the children who would suffer the most. Her fantasies could go on, but in real life she needed to focus on providing for Gabriella and Sophia, not on the gorgeous SEAL in front of her.

Chapter Seven

Mac was adjusting to fatherhood with an ease he hadn't expected, despite the fact the twins never slept through the night. He was developing a bond with them that he hadn't thought possible with a child that wasn't his own. It brought a whole new understanding to what Nicole went through; he could resonate with her fears that they'd be taken away from her. She was a wonderful mother to them, and he couldn't have asked for someone better to be on this path to parenthood with him.

Though the twins took up most of their time, he couldn't get her out of his mind. Every thought seemed to center around her, his gaze following her wherever she went. For the first time, possibly ever, he wanted to get to know a woman—Nicole. It wasn't just about getting her into bed, even though he did want her badly. He needed *more* with her. If it was just about sex, he could have gotten that from anyone else. Nicole would need more, too. She wasn't a woman who would take anything less than a commitment.

Stay away from her; you don't need that. You're a SEAL, you can't give a commitment. With the internal warning bells going off, he couldn't stop himself from gazing down the path that would lead them together. The way she inquired if there was someone waiting in Virginia for him was enough of an indication that she was interested in him. All he had to do was make his move.

Shawn had always had a sixth sense about things, even his own death. Could he have believed that bringing them together would give Gabriella and Sophia a real family again? Still, he doubted that he could give Nicole what she deserved. She warranted only the best, someone who didn't have baggage and scars. He had already seen how she reacted to the scars on his chest; if she saw his back, it would only be worse. He couldn't stand the sorrow in her sparkling blue eyes.

"Mr. Batty is here," Nicole whispered from the doorway.

"I'll be right out." He took one last look at the sleeping girls before leaving the nursery. For the sake of the twins, he'd find a way to balance things with Nicole. They didn't need the additional tension if things didn't work out.

There's plenty of other women...but not like her. He knew without a doubt she was one of a kind. Images of the sashay of her hips filled his head and hardened his shaft. She was beautiful, so full of life and love. In just a few short days, she'd gotten under his skin, so much that he couldn't think straight. He needed to pull himself together. At any moment, duty could call, and a distraction could get him killed. His men depended on him having his head on straight, not distracted by a woman, especially not one he was denying himself of.

He stepped into the living room and wondered why he was denying himself her physical company. The excuses he gave himself were just that. If he wanted her bad enough, they'd find a way to make it work.

"Lieutenant Commander García, it is nice to finally meet you." Mr. Batty stood and held out his hand as Mac came around the sofa.

"Please call me Mac." He took the lawyer's hand, returning the firm handshake.

"Nicole has been filling me in on your plans to return to Virginia together. I think a trial run before the paperwork is drawn up would be the best way to test out joint custody. It will also give her a chance to check out Virginia and your lifestyle."

"Raising the girls together seems like the perfect way for us. She loves them, and they need that." Mac sat down on the sofa and laid his hand over Nicole's. "Going to Virginia for the holidays will give her a good insight to military life. The Christmas parties will allow her to meet my men and their wives, as well as other military families, without pressure. As you said, it's a good introduction into the life."

"Very well. Then if you'll keep me updated, I can draw up the paperwork when you're ready. After the New Year, we can also finalize the house, Shawn's business transactions, and other documents. Merry Christmas." Mr. Batty rose from the chair he had been sitting in and grabbed his briefcase. "I'm very sorry for your loss, for both of you. Shawn was a good man. He had an excellent business mind and has made sure the children will have a secure future."

"Thank you." When Mac first pulled up to the house, he wondered what Shawn had done to afford an estate like this. Careers were one thing they'd never discussed; it just never came up, and Mac had never wanted to share the details of his own life. "I'll see you out." He rose from the sofa and led the way to the door.

"I appreciate you coming to us." Nicole called after the lawyer before he could get out of hearing range. "I'd have called you and saved you the trip, but with the girls' allergic reaction, I forgot about it."

"There's no problem, Nicole. I'm happy the two of you have worked something out. If you need anything, you have my number." Mr. Batty stopped by the living room entry.

"Thank you. I believe it's all going to work out. We'll be in touch. Enjoy the holidays and try not to work too hard."

Mac listened to Nicole and Mr. Batty's exchange, but only one comment actually mattered. She was optimistic. Knowing she was on board and looking forward to what the future held gave him hope. It was going to be a bumpy road for both of them, maybe more for her than him, because when he was back on duty, caring for the children would fall on her.

The lawyer paused before he left, glancing toward the living room. "I received notification this morning that a cottage was purchased by Shawn the day he died. He has already given the owner a check, but with the circumstances, I might be able to get you out of it if you'd prefer. Or I can arrange to put it back on the market." He kept his voice low and Mac wondered if he knew the importance of the cottage to Nicole.

"No." He glanced back toward the living room. "Do what needs to be done, I want it to go into Nicole's name. It's hers."

"Okay. I'll be in touch." Mr. Batty stepped outside and tugged his coat closer. Even in Texas, the cold winter air beat against them. "Take good care of Nicole and the girls, they mean a lot to everyone in this town."

"I will. Small towns are hard to find anymore, but don't worry…we'll be back. I have no plans to sell the house, so if you know of anyone who'd be willing to keep it maintained while I'm in Virginia, please let me know."

Mr. Batty nodded before turning to go back to his car. Mac stood there a moment longer, letting the cold seep into his body and chase away his burning desire for Nicole that never seemed to dissipate.

"Wow, the wind makes it colder." He hadn't heard Nicole come up behind him until she spoke.

"What did Shawn do for a living?" He turned to her, wondering how his nephew had afforded the house, cottage, and a comfortable nest egg for the girls.

"Shawn was an investor." The mention of Shawn's name brought a distant look to her eyes. "He put money into start-up companies, and if they paid off he made out well. If they didn't, they still had to pay back the money that was used. He was a genius when it came to business. His investments will transfer to you, to continue to provide financial support for the twins. The last few months I've straightened out his bookkeeping, so you shouldn't have to worry about providing for the girls, even if they want to get doctoral degrees at Ivy League universities."

"I'm not concerned about money to raise the girls. Whatever is there will be saved for them—for their colleges, their futures." He slipped his hand in hers. "Come sit, I want to ask you something."

"Something worse than picking up and moving across country?" She teased, but came away from the door with him.

He couldn't think of anything lighthearted enough to say, so he remained quiet until they made it to the sofa. What he had to know might be worse for her depending on the answer. It might bring up hard feelings or worse yet, the ghost of his nephew. He still wasn't sure how he felt about the possibility that there could have been more between Nicole and Shawn than friendship and a working relationship. If she had feelings for his nephew, would that change what was starting to develop between them?

"Mac, you've turned serious, what's going on?"

"You asked me before if there was a woman waiting for me back in Virginia." He paused as they sank down onto the sofa. "When you talk about Shawn, there's a longing in your eyes—"

"Where is this going?" She interrupted him before he could get his thought out.

"I need to know if there was anything between the two of you."

"I can't believe you." She pulled her hand out of his grasp and leaned back against the sofa. "You think I was screwing Shawn?"

"Nicole." He reached out to take hold of her hand again but she pulled farther away. "When you speak of Shawn there seemed to be a deep longing, more than I expected there to be between you two. I just need to know where things stood between you, how deep the feelings go."

"Why?"

How the hell am I supposed to answer that? He could have sworn she could see what's happening between them. Was it just on his part, or did she feel something toward him too? It had been too long since he had any sort of attraction toward a woman, so maybe he was off his game. All these years he kept his emotions out of the picture when it came to women, keeping his commitments to only the night or a few days while he was on leave. She was throwing him off balance.

"Answer me," she demanded, cutting through his thoughts.

"I need to know…because if you loved him, that could change whatever is happening between us."

"I did love him, but not in the way you're thinking. Shawn became my best friend, another brother. The girls were preemie because of their mother's unfortunate accident. We spent many hours sitting in the nursery, just holding the girls, giving them the comfort they needed. It gave us time to talk, to really get to know each other." She wiped the tears away that had begun to fall. "What you see is sadness, longing, and grief. I'm questioning fate, and everything that people believe in, because I don't understand how two helpless infants could be brought into a loving family, a family who had been trying so long to have children, only to have it all snatched away from them before their first birthday. I'm not sure that's the world I want to see more life brought into. If the girls have already handled this much heartache, what is the rest of their life going to be like?"

"I've been in a similar position where I've questioned the reason things happened. It leaves you with an emptiness in the pit of your stomach. It's not a place I'd like to be again." He had been to the point of wondering if it was all worth it, not long ago.

"Why?" She leaned closer to him, almost as if she was going to touch him. "What brought you to that place and how did you get past it? Right now it feels like the world will never be the same."

"It will until you force yourself to look at the positives. Shawn is gone, but if you believe he's still watching over the girls, then he's not that far away. As for what brought me out of the depression, it was my men. They depend on me to have my head in the action, and if I can't I'm going to get them killed." *More of them killed,* he silently corrected.

"You didn't answer my entire question."

"I know." He stood from the sofa and put distance between them. "That's a story for another time." Or *never* if he had his way. He didn't need her to hear that he'd failed his men. That two of them were dead and another had lost his leg on a mission. He didn't want to see the same look of disappointment in her eyes he saw in everyone else's, or the grief he had witnessed with the widows.

"I bare my soul but you get to brush me aside, is that how this works? If you won't talk to me, how am I supposed to trust you? One thing Shawn never did was treat me as a lesser being because I was the twins' nanny, and I won't stand for you to do that to me either."

"I'm not." He ran a hand over his head, feeling the buzz cut under his fingers. "What do you want me to say? I led my men into an ambush, two of them were killed on-site, and a third is now an amputee because of my decision. That's what sent me down the spiral of doubt. Will that make you sleep better tonight, knowing I failed them?"

"Mac—"

"Don't." Without looking back, he headed for the door. "I need some air." He had to get away from her before he made things worse, or before he could see what he expected to find in her eyes. There was no way he could stand to look at her every day if she thought he was a failure.

Most of the time, his men didn't look at him that way, but it didn't stop the guilt from that day affecting every decision he made on missions. Next time, he could get them all killed and he couldn't allow that. He had a duty to bring his team home; each of them had someone waiting for them. It wasn't just Ace and Boom's wives and children, each of his men had family and friends. People who would need him to look into their eyes and tell them what happened. He couldn't, *wouldn't*, do it again. He'd bring his men home, or he'd die on the battlefield with them.

Chapter Eight

Cold to the very core, Nicole was unsure how to handle Mac's outburst. She wanted to go to him, but at the same time she couldn't help but feel as if this was a battle they had to cross before anything could develop between them. They needed to be on solid footing for a friendship, for any kind of relationship. Lies or secrets would only make things more difficult further down the line.

What the hell am I doing? I'm only the girls' nanny, that's all he'll see me as. He only wants me in Virginia so he can stay a SEAL. She cursed herself for thinking she might be able to have a relationship with him. She was far too geeky once men started to get to know her, and she never attracted men like *that*. There was no doubt in her mind. Men like Mac went after cute little blondes with perky breasts, and stick figure bodies. That was something she could never compete with—her brown hair and eye combination was nothing spectacular, but it was the curvy figure that also pushed men away. She learned long ago some men didn't appreciate a body that had what her grandmother called *childbearing hips*, extra curves, and a little more to love.

Friendship was all she could hope for with Mac, and it was what they needed in order to raise the girls together. She rose from the sofa, grabbed the baby monitor, and with determination, set out to find him. Before she finished packing for Virginia, she had to let him know that she was sorry. She wasn't sure why it mattered so much that she had to do it then, instead of waiting until he had time to cool off, but everything in her told her she needed to do it now. That he had to know that his confession didn't change things.

She didn't even make it around the sofa before her cell phone started to vibrate in her pocket. Tempted to ignore it, she took another step before she forced herself to at least look at the caller ID. *Mom.*

Shit. She knew what her mom was calling about and the calls wouldn't stop until she answered. It was better to get it over with while Mac wasn't around, so she slid her finger over the screen and brought it to her ear. "Hi, Mom."

"I'm sure the guardian who was appointed for those children has arrived. When are you coming home?" With no *hello* or *how are you*, her mother cut straight to the point.

"I'm not." She leaned against the back of the sofa. "I'm going to be away for a while."

"What?" Her mother's voice rose another octave.

"I'm going to Virginia with the girls' guardian to help. It's a hard time for them right now, and this will make it easier for them." She didn't explain that it might be a permanent solution.

"I don't know what's gotten into you, girl, you gave up your successful career to care for some screaming brats. You're ruining your life." Her mother let out a deep sign. "It's time you get your head out of the clouds, get back to work. Then you can find a man and have a family of your own instead of raising children who don't even belong to you."

"Mom, I hated being an accountant."

"Then get married, have a bunch of babies, and stay home. Don't go running off to help another man raise his unless you're going to marry him." She let her mother ramble on about how it was a woman's place to marry and have children, and tried not to hold it against her. It was how she was raised, and there was no changing her mother.

That was all she cared about, making Nicole an honest woman. Since the day she gave up her practice and moved in with Shawn there had been tension between them. The day Shawn died, her mother didn't give her sympathies, or ask if there was anything her or the girls needed, instead all she wanted to know was when Nicole was moving back home.

Well, it wasn't happening, even if things didn't work out in Virginia. She would never go back to her hometown and begin her accounting practice again. In just a few short months, this had become her home. If she had to rebuild her life, she'd do it here.

I can't think about it falling apart, this is my chance to stay in the girls' lives. It's what I want, and I'm not going so I can be near Mac…he's just an added bonus.

The Texas air was bone chilling in a way Mac hadn't expected. When he thought of Texas, the first thing that came to mind was the heat, and even after all his years of traveling, Texas was one state he hadn't marked off the list. With less than two weeks until Christmas, he didn't expect to feel the same chill in the air as he did in Virginia. The air felt cold enough to snow, but that was rare, wasn't it?

He sunk down on the steps of the porch and pulled out his phone. *Christmas.* Guilt, regret, and undying sadness poured through him. The first Christmas alone for the families of the two SEALs he'd gotten killed. He flicked through the pictures on his phone until he found the one of the men together, taken just days before the mission that changed the team forever.

The minute they stepped out of their Humvee and headed to the door of what they were told was an informant's house, the gunfire erupted all around them. There had been no safe place to take cover and the vehicle was too far. They hunkered down the best they could and returned fire. Every time they took out an insurgent, two more took its place. A fucking setup, and they were on their own. No backup was coming to get them out of the ambush they'd walked into. After twenty years in the military, he should have known better. Faulty intelligence got two of his men killed, another disabled, but it could have got them all killed.

"Commander..." The urgency in Bad Billy's tone cut through the gunfire.

Mac had turned his head enough to glance at Bad Billy from the corner of his eye, and what he saw sent a new rush of anger through him. "Fuck!" He grabbed James's ballistic vest and tugged him closer to the wall. Blood stained the ground around them red. "Rebel!"

"I got him, Sir." The team's medic, Rebel, pulled his pack out and reached for the tourniquet first. "Stay with us, James, you hear me? Stay with us." His tone held insistence; it was a demand, as if to tell James he had no other choice but to live. He hurriedly tied off the arteries to cut the blood flow.

"Goddamn it, don't you fucking die on me." Mac looked around to assess the damage to his team. Two were missing. "Where's—" He didn't finish his sentence before Bad Billy pointed farther down the line.

"Britt is in a bad place, but Rebel did what he could."

He glanced at Britt's pale face. "Ace, Boom, get a smoke screen ready. We've got to get back to the Humvee. Rebel, can you move him?"

"Don't see a choice, Commander." Rebel threw his equipment back in his pack.

"Whiskey and I will get the others." Bad Billy grabbed the fallen member of the team, leaving Whiskey to grab Britt.

"Let's go." Mac nodded to Ace and Boom who had the smoke grenades ready.

"Mac?" A soft female voice called through his thoughts. "Hey, are you okay?" She laid a hand on his shoulder and it took him a moment to realize it was Nicole.

"Fine." He closed his eyes and forced the memories back in the bottle he kept them in, stored away where they didn't haunt him every second of the day.

"I wanted to apologize. I didn't mean to upset you, I just didn't know." She leaned against the pillar, her gaze on the ground instead of looking at him.

"Don't worry about it." He slid his thumb over the screen and brought the picture back up. "I failed my men, but I won't fail you or the girls. That you have to believe."

"I don't believe you failed them. Just in the few days you've been here I know you're not the type of man who would be careless. You did everything you could to bring everyone home safe and in one piece." She brushed against his shoulder with her fingertips, rubbing along the collarbone. "No one understands the cost of war better than the troops, but you have to remember what we're fighting for. What your men died for."

"What's that? Honestly, some days I wonder if I even know what we're fighting for anymore. Even when the country isn't at war, there's always some mission. It *should* be to keep our country safe, but it seems like every time we make our land a little safer, another threat pops up. Will we ever have a safe world for Gabriella and Sophia to be raised in?" He tipped his head, pressing the side of his face against the back of her hand. "Even after losing my men, I didn't doubt we were fighting for a better future. Now I look at those two little girls and think of how many children have lost their parents because of war." *What if I'm the next casualty?*

"No one understands the losses more than you and the others who serve, but in the end, isn't our country worth it? Nine-eleven started this latest battle, and lives have been destroyed and lost, but that doesn't mean what we're doing is wrong. I've seen the protestors as the funerals, but I've also seen the patriot guard riders who form a guard around the families to keep the harassment at bay. You can't tell me what you do isn't worth it. You keep dangers at bay that we don't even know about. That's honorable and courageous."

"*Amore.*" It slipped out before he could stop it. What was he thinking calling her *love?* She was too young for him. Instead of letting his mind take over, he pressed his lips to the back of her hand, gently placing a kiss there. "You have the heart of a saint, but you have no idea what you're getting into. Do you?"

"I don't, but I'm about to dive in head-first." She gave him an easy smile. "That doesn't change things, I'm still committed to it."

He let the silence fall over them like a comfortable blanket, just enjoying the moment with her, trying not to question the future he couldn't change. If the military life was too hard on her, he was willing to step back and let her bring the girls back to Texas. She'd raise them and he'd be as involved as he could. It was the right thing to do, not only because of his career but also because of her love for the babies. His life had always been about doing the right thing, no matter the cost or personal discomfort, and this would be no different.

"García is Italian, and so is *amore*...but you don't look it."

"You mean my blond hair and blue eyes makes you doubt I'm Italian?" He joked. "I was adopted at birth, my adoptive parents were Italian. It throws people off guard, when they hear Mac García they expect someone with deep olive skin and dark hair."

"Do you speak Italian then?"

"My parents made sure I could speak their language. I'm bilingual, and would like to raise the girls the same way. If you'd like I can teach you."

"I'm not a very good student. In order to graduate high school I had to take two years of a foreign language, mine was Spanish. Let's just say if it wasn't for my teacher taking pity on me I would have never have made it out of school."

"The way you learn in a high school class is basic words and it can be detrimental for some. It can be easier learning in real life situation." The thought of high school reminded him of the age difference between them. *What the hell was I thinking? Why would she be interested in an old man like me?*

"I'd like to try, but you've been warned."

"Nicole, how old are you?"

She sat down next to him, stretching her long legs out in front of him. "Didn't your mama teach you it's impolite to ask a woman her age?"

"She'd wash my mouth out with soap if she knew, but sometimes you have to be indelicate to make sure you're not making a mistake."

"Mistake on my age, or a mistake on the desire you mention earlier?" She cocked her head to the side, her gaze on him.

"You're making this harder than it needs to be." With a deep sigh, he rubbed the arch of his nose. "I'm an old man set in my ways and no matter how desirable I find you that doesn't change things."

"I'm twenty-four." She kept her tone soft, as if she didn't want to say it out loud.

"*Merda.*" What was he thinking, letting her get into his thoughts as she had? She was the twins' nanny, a possible friend, nothing more. He couldn't think of getting involved with her.

"Mac, age isn't anything but a number." She pressed her hand to his thigh, giving it a squeeze.

"I'll be forty in January. That's sixteen years' difference. A lifetime." *Damn it. Why did I have to make myself sound older? I couldn't just say thirty-nine. No, I had to make it the big four-zero.* He'd been learning to drive when she was born. It was insane to even think about them together. Damn, he needed to get out of here and back to Virginia. His work would keep her out of his thoughts; a mission would put distance between them. Too bad he promised his team no training until after the New Year, and hopefully no missions would interrupt the holidays. They deserved the downtime, even if he'd kill for something to call him away from Nicole, so he could rebuild the walls that had to separate them.

You cannot get involved with her.

Chapter Nine

The tension that had developed between them had Nicole ready to scream. She'd have lied about her age if she had known Mac would react this way. Why did age have to play into anything? She could feel the attraction between them and he had already admitted it, so why did he put up barriers? She had tried to talk to him before they left for the airport but the girls had gotten up earlier than expected, and then they had to be on their way.

It wasn't something she had wanted to discuss on the plane, not that they could have. Traveling with the girls had been as much of a nightmare as she expected, and the flight had been the worst part. Now all that was left was the drive to his house, and then maybe she could have a quiet moment with him after they got the girls settled and fed.

"Since my truck doesn't have room for the baby seats, I arranged for my dad to bring his car over and take my truck this morning. I also called Mr. Batty before we left. He said he'd make sure Shawn's SUV was shipped for you. Should be here in a week if we're lucky. In the meantime, Dad said we could use this one."

"Won't he need it?"

"He can use Mom's if he needs to, or he can have my truck. We'll work it out." He steered the luggage cart toward a red mid-size four-door car. "I should warn you, they've already told me they'll be over tomorrow to meet the girls."

The idea of meeting his parents set butterflies loose in her stomach. "It will be nice that the girls will have additional family, though they've never been around many people since they've been born."

"They're about to get their first dose of family." He lifted Sophia's car seat from the stroller and went around to the other side of the car. "Some of my team is at the house."

"What?"

"I checked my voicemail while you were in the restroom changing Gabriella, and they left a message. I didn't expect them to stick around after the task but they did." He ducked his head inside the car and buckled the car seat in without waking Sophia. "I'll get rid of them as soon as I can."

"How many are we talking?" she whispered, repeating his motions with Gabriella's car seat.

"Ace, Boom, and their wives. Maybe Bad Billy."

She swallowed, thankful it was only five not a whole group. "How many men do you command?"

"My squad is made up of seven men, eight if you include me. Ace and Boom are the only two married. Boom is actually married to Ace's sister Wynn." He walked around to the back of the car where he parked the luggage cart and begin to load the trunk. "I called them because between Gwen and Wynn were sure to get the house to a point where we could bring the girls home. Ace and Gwen have a daughter the same age, and Wynn would be able to get what I asked her to, since with her boutiques she has the connections."

"What did you ask them to do?" She grabbed the diaper bag from the top of the cart and placed it on the floor in the backseat.

"You'll have to wait until we get there, I don't like to spoil surprises." He laid the stroller on top of the bags and shut the trunk.

"I'm not much for surprises." She eyed him over the roof of the car.

"Too bad." He smirked and for the first time since the age issue came up there seemed to be a relaxed moment between them.

"Should I expect a house like a typical bachelor? Pizza boxes, beer bottles, clothes tossed everywhere."

He waited to answer until they got into the car and he put it in gear. "No, I'm a clean bachelor, plus since I was just on a training exercise I haven't been there in two weeks."

She relaxed against the stiff seat as he pulled out of the airport parking lot, knowing she'd have her work cut out for her. Not only would she have to deal with his friends, she'd have to clean the house. She doubted after two weeks things would be clean enough to set up a temporary nursery. The next few days were going to be long and trying. Tonight she'd have to set up a temporary bed for the girls in the portable playpen, but then they'd have to get cribs and other baby supplies tomorrow.

For a fleeting moment, she thought of Mac's friend who owned the baby boutiques, wondering if he'd asked her to bring something. Even if he had, knowing how expensive this stuff was, she doubted Wynn would bring much of anything.

"You're worrying too much." He glanced at her as he pulled into traffic, leaving the airport behind them. "Your forehead is all scrunched up, it's a clear sign. There's no training exercise until after the New Year and unless we're called for a mission I'll be here to help you adjust. It's going to be fine."

"There's just so much we need to do in order to get the girls settled and I know they aren't going to make this easy. They've been through so much lately, and this move has just increased the tension. They need things to calm down, a secure life without the ups and downs they've had so far."

"We're going to give them that." He took her hand in his and laced their fingers together. "Everything is going to work out and the girls are going to be happy and healthy. They'll love Virginia and so will you. You'll see. We'll make this Christmas something special...for all of us."

"Us?"

"This is a new beginning, it should be special."

She wasn't sure how to take that comment but she'd had about enough of the mixed signals to last a lifetime. Either he was interested in her as something more than just a means to keep his career and the girls, or he wasn't. If he wasn't, he shouldn't be intertwining their fingers and making comments that hinted at more one moment, and nothing the next. Her heart could take rejection, but not repeatedly.

Maybe making the journey to Virginia to be with him and the girls was a mistake. It seemed like a good thing for the babies, but what was it doing to her future? She was putting her life and the possibility of love on hold in order to raise them with a man who could never look at her as more than just a nanny. Her mother might have been right when she told Nicole to wise up and think of her own life.

Someday she wanted a husband and children of her own. She wouldn't get that if she was in a going nowhere agreement with Mac to raise Gabriella and Sophia. She just wasn't sure she had the strength to walk away from the two little girls who captured her heart and brought meaning back into her life.

"We're here." Mac announced as he pulled into the driveway of a huge French colonial.

It was everything she pictured and more, the rectangular, symmetrical design, with all the classic features of the style: five windows across the front, a raised basement, exterior stairs, full-length porch and a large roof that covered the porch. The antique white house with mahogany trim around the windows, doors, balcony, and pillars. Even with the work that still needed to be done it was grand. A true gem that deserved to be brought back to its former glory.

"It's beautiful!"

"It's come a long way since I purchased it and there's still tons to do but it's home." He continued down the long driveway. As they neared the house, she noticed it wasn't just one exterior staircase but actually two that met in the middle allowing someone to come up on either side of the house. "When I bought the house, I had considered flipping it but now that I've put so much work into it I can't picture selling it. With six bedrooms, it was too big for me, but now with you and the girls it will feel like a home."

"Six bedrooms," she exclaimed, unable to believe it.

"There's also a library, home office, and my favorite part...a home theater." The car came to a stop between an SUV and a large truck. "I bet you're wondering why and how."

"A little. Mostly why...why would you want a house so large for just you?"

"Dad had his own construction business until he sold it two years ago, and every day on his way home he'd pass this place. He saw the potential in it and was drawn to it. When it went on the market I purchased it, hoping it would be something we'd be able to restore together. I had hoped to give it to them, and take their house since it's closer to the base. I thought they'd enjoy it, but Dad refused. He said it was too much house for them, and that I would need it one day. He said I'd have a family of my own and could raise my children here."

"Guess he was right."

"Looks like they've spotted us." He tipped his head to the steps as a woman came down. "That's Ace's wife Gwen, they have a daughter named Roulette who's the same age as the girls."

"Playdates." She suggested it not only for the girls, but because it would be nice to have another woman helping her adjust to military life. "Let's get the girls inside before they catch a chill."

She opened her door and stepped out, her gaze going to the back seat where Gabriella and Sophia slept peacefully. They'd end up paying for the nap this close to bedtime but for the brief peacefulness it was worth it.

"You must be Nicole, I'm Gwen." She held her hand out.

"Where are my men?" Mac asked as he came around the car with Sophia. "I thought I'd put them to work to carry in the luggage."

"They just delivered what you asked and had to go help Whiskey. Wynn is upstairs doing the final touches, why don't I handle the girls and you go show Nicole what you arranged." Without waiting for an answer, Gwen opened the car door and leaned in to unhook Gabriella's car seat.

"I can do that." Nicole tried to argue but it was no use.

"Come on, Gwen is a natural." He slipped his free arm around Nicole's waist. "If I make it inside with Sophia sleeping I'll put her car seat in the living room and we'll be down in a few minutes."

"Take your time." Gwen fell into step a few feet behind with Gabriella and the diaper bag.

"What did you do?" Nicole asked as they made their way up the exterior steps.

"The girls needed a nursery, so I asked Gwen and Wynn for help to get them settled in tonight. It's just the basics but it will give them a place to sleep that isn't a playpen." He opened one of the French front doors and ushered her inside. "Come on, I want to see what they've done."

Anticipation churned her stomach as they made their way up the grand staircase just off the living room. "I know it's been a long day but once we're alone and the girls are asleep, we need to talk."

"As long as I can have a cold beer, I'll do whatever you ask." He paused at the top of the steps. "You lead the way. It's the last door on the right, sandwiched between the master bedroom and what I thought could be yours."

"Here I thought I'd get to choose which of the five spare bedrooms I wanted." She joked as she strolled down the hallway.

"You're more than welcome to pick another room and I'll be sure to get it done for you quickly. Right now, the room I offered you and the nursery were the only two bedrooms complete. After the master, the bedrooms were low on my priority list."

"I was just teasing, anywhere is fine with me. It's better that I'm close to the girls anyway." She reached out, about to wrap her hand around the door handle before it flew opened.

"Oh." A pregnant woman with shoulder length blonde hair stepped back. "I was just going to tell Gwen to send you up, things are ready. By the way, I'm Wynn."

"Nicole." It came out shallow but her thoughts were elsewhere. The nursery was beautiful. The warm butterscotch walls with white wainscot set off the ebony cribs as if it were planned. The large window cast streaks of the early evening sun around the room.

"I know it's not everything you need, but we did our best in the time we had."

"You did more than I expected. Thank you," Mac told Wynn while Nicole neared the ebony rockers that sat near the cribs.

"It's beautiful. The cribs with the etchings on the railings, it's stunning."

"If you look carefully you can see there are flags and stars mixed in with the swirl design. It's the independence model, only carried at Heart of Diamond, my children's boutique. They will transform into toddler beds when the time comes," Wynn explained.

"The changing table, dressers, and rockers match. The details are amazing. Thank you." Nicole ran her fingers over every surface.

"Don't thank me, it was all Mac. I just set it up."

"The nursery couldn't have come together without you, Gwen, Ace, and Boom, I do appreciate it." Something in Mac's tone had Nicole glancing back at him to find him smiling at her.

Wynn laid her hand on Mac's arm, and it sent an unexpected wave of jealousy through Nicole. "You've had a long day of traveling and I know you need to get the girls settled, so we'll take off. Nicole, I look forward to meeting you again and if you need anything Mac knows how to reach us. If my boutique doesn't have it I have the connections to find whatever you need."

"Thank you."

"I'll see you out." Mac followed Wynn, leaving Nicole in the nursery alone.

She stood by the window, her knees brushing against the window seat as she tried to remind herself she had no reason to be jealous. Mac wasn't hers and never would be. If she was going to stick around and raise the girls with him, she couldn't react like a knife had been stabbed through her chest every time a woman was around.

Eventually he'd find someone to date, possibly marry, and she'd have to deal with that. She knew he wasn't interested in her; she was too young. So why did it hurt to see another woman, even a married woman, touch him?

He's mine.

She tried to force the thought away, knowing it wasn't true—and never would be.

Chapter Ten

With a cold beer in his hand, Mac leaned against the granite countertop with Wynn's parting words replaying in his mind.

She's just the woman you need. Don't let her slip through your fingers, treat her right, and everything will work out. Enjoy your Christmas break, Commander. Dating advice was not what he needed, but maybe she was right.

She was sixteen years his junior, and he still believed age would eventually become a problem. It didn't stop him from wanting her. What would her parents say about it? His parents? Nearly forty and he still worried about what his parents were going to say. He was fortunate enough to have a close bond with them. His father had told them once that he saved them, but to him it was the other way around. He heard the horror stories of what the state childcare system was like and his parents had rescued him from that. They had given him a home and love when they didn't have to.

He had done with the girls what his parents had done for him, and now he finally understood what his dad meant. Gabriella and Sophia brought a new meaning to his life, one that wasn't just the military. Their smiles first thing in the morning when they were still sleepy, and he picked them up out of the crib. Those were the moments when it was all worth everything. He realized what he did was truly worth it; his career kept his babies safe. That made it worth every loss.

"The girls are asleep." Nicole sat the baby monitor on the countertop and flopped onto one of the bar stools, exhausted. "Do you have any more of those?"

"Wynn left you a bottle of wine chilling if you'd prefer."

"No, beer is fine."

He stepped away from the counter, grabbed another beer bottle from the refrigerator, and cracked it open before handing it to her. "You wanted to talk."

"I do." She took a long drink of the beer. "Mac, you're a great guy—"

"But you're old." He cut her off and filled in the blank because he knew where this was going. So much for Wynn's encouragement.

"No." She sat the beer on the counter with a thump, sending the liquid inside sloshing out. "That wasn't what I was going to say at all. I wanted to talk to you about the mixed signals. You said yesterday that nothing could happen between us because I'm too young for you, then today you give me hope that you've changed your mind. Mac, for us to raise the girls together without tension between us I can't go back and forth. Either you have no intentions on exploring this attraction or you do, but you can't have it both ways. You can't slip your arm around my waist and pull me against your body one minute and then turn the cold tap the next."

"Do you not think there will be comments about our age difference?"

"Who the hell cares? This is our life. We're the ones who need to be happy. Are you worried the general public won't approve, or your commanding officers? Are you implying there could be career consequences?"

"This isn't about my career, it's about us." He pushed off the counter, crossing the space in two quick steps, and laid his hand over hers. "You're young, with your whole life ahead of you. Do you really want to settle for an old man? You could have children of your own with a man who will be there for your lifetime."

"Our time here isn't guaranteed, if anyone knows that it's us. Right now, I want you. As for tomorrow, next week, or even next year, who knows? We'll have to take things as they come. I think we should explore this and see where it leads." She slipped off the bar stool and came around the bar to stand before him. "You're not old, mature but not old, and as I said before...age means nothing to me."

"Age plays a part in things more than you know." He wrapped his arms around her waist. "Someday I'll leave you as a widow."

"That's something I'll have to deal with. Or it could be the other way around, just as it happened with Shawn." She pressed her body along the length of him, making his resistance drop another level.

"You're beautiful." He tangled his hand in her hair and gazed into her eyes, which held disbelief. "Utterly beautiful. Tomorrow I'm going to take away your doubt."

"Why tomorrow, when I'm right here waiting?" Her voice remained low and timid.

Every part of him wanted to take her, to have her in every way possible, but not tonight. They both had a long few days, and the traveling had taken its toll on them. Tonight she should go to bed alone and think about where things were going. "I want you to have one last night to think about what it will mean if we go down this path. You need to understand what challenges we will face. Not just with our age difference, but with my career, the girls, the mystery and loneliness that a relationship with me might leave you with."

"Loneliness?" She raised an eyebrow at him.

"I don't just mean while I'm deployed. Military wives are great support, but the SEAL group is small tightknit family. SEALs make up less than one percent of the Navy. The only two married in my squad are Ace and Boom. Hell, even my commander isn't married, he doesn't have a life outside of work. That's been me for years, and change won't happen overnight." He let his finger slide under the edge of her sweater to tease along the edge of her jeans, against her bare flesh.

"You are who you are, I'm not asking you to change." She cupped his cheek. "You worry too much...just like me."

"I'm trained to think of all the outcomes, to weigh the possibilities; I can't turn it off even when I want to." He took a step back, taking her with him until his back was against the counter again. "Another possibility I've been considering, you've always had Shawn there with the girls when you've needed additional help. If I'm training or on a mission I won't be here to help, what do you think about hiring a nanny to help you?"

"A nanny?" Her head tipped back in pure laughter. "*I'm* supposed to be the nanny," she reminded him between bouts of giggles.

"I think we both know that you're more than just a nanny to those girls. You're their mother, and after the holidays I plan to make it official. No matter what happens between us, you should be their guardian. We'll be their parents, but I have to say those poor girls got saddled with the short end of the deal, having me as their father."

"You've been a wonderful father to the girls. Gabriella and Sophia have taken to you like I never expected." She pressed a light kiss to his chin. "We're making a family for the girls and things will turn out fine."

He wasn't sure what fine was when it came to him being a father, or having this instant family, but he'd learned long ago to go with the flow. As long as Nicole stuck by him through the learning curve, things would turn out okay. She had been his rock through all of this, assisting him when he was at a loss with what the girls wanted. Age difference or not, he realized while he was pretending to sleep through the flights, when the girls weren't fussing, that he wasn't willing to give her up. He'd do what he could to prove he wasn't some old fella, and the first step was doing something special for her.

Tomorrow.

With Mac on the phone and the girls tucked into their crib, Nicole took one last look around the kitchen. The gray and silver swirled granite countertops set nicely against the cherry wood cabinets and high-end appliances. The black back-splash, with silver accents, tied everything together. The gourmet kitchen was beyond what she'd have expected him to put in the house when he said it only cooked the basics. But if he was going to flip the house, this kitchen would get the most bang for the buck. She could picture herself cooking in the space, making them dinners while the girls played in the living area off the kitchen.

What she had seen of the house so far, she could see it being a home to them. A place where the girls could grow and she could start a new life with Mac. Things were moving quicker in her mind than physically, but she knew that somehow they would work things out. They'd be together in the end, giving the girls a true family in every way, and possibly someday adding to their little family.

With one last glance at the kitchen, she made her way down the hall and through the rest of the downstairs. Exploring each room as she came to it and trying to picture what Mac had started. Many of the rooms were untouched, or only half-finished, but the living room and kitchen were complete. Even with all the work he had already done there was still a lot left to do. Just on the main floor there was still the dining room, den, library, and second family room. Upstairs he still had six bedrooms, not including the basement he mentioned wanting to finish to create an entertaining paradise to go along with the home theater that was already down there. The basement would be an entertainer's dream since it opened up nicely to the patio in the back.

She had grown up in a small house with hardworking parents, but money had always been tight, so when she first saw Shawn's house she fell in love with it. The grandness of it all had been overwhelming, but it was just the idea of having space to spread out, not having to be on top of one another. After sharing a room with her brother until she moved out, she loved having a space she could call her own.

At Shawn's she had turned her bedroom into a retreat, a place just for her where she could go to relax and unwind. She hadn't even seen her bedroom here but she already knew she didn't need it. There were plenty of places for her to unwind, her favorite already being the library with its window seat overlooking the back yard. Maybe she could convince him to work on that room before the others.

She stood there looking down on the yard. The flagstone patio dominated the space right behind the house, with bright green grass until the property backed to nothing put trees as far as the eye could see. Peaceful privacy and over six acres of it.

"I was thinking of adding a large custom-built swing and play-set for the girls." Mac came up behind her, placing a hand on her lower back.

"You do know they won't be able to use it for a while, right?"

"I was thinking baby swings, and I can change them out later. It's a thought, but not until the weather is nicer. In the meantime, I can get the house in order. I need to finish things before we have them walking around."

"I was just thinking about that. Maybe you could push this room up your to-do list?" She turned so her body was almost against him. "It's such a cozy room. I can see the girls and me spending time in here. I see them quietly playing in front of the fire and I know I could spend hours on this window seat lost in a novel."

"*Amore*, as you command. Also, a guest room in case you wish to invite family or friends for a visit."

Her stomach rolled and she stepped back out of his touch and dropped down onto the hardwood window seat. She loved her mother but the idea of having her invade this haven made Nicole sick. Her mother didn't understand what she was doing with her life, and the idea of Nicole spending her life raising someone else's children was appalling to her.

"No…no one will be visiting."

"You're more than welcome to have anyone here." His brows creased in confusion.

"No." She tucked a strand of her hair behind her ear. "My parents don't understand, and after the latest call from my mother I don't want her here. If I want to see them, I'll go to Texas. My brother Sam and I are close, but he hates to travel, so there's no reason to think he'd come even if I invited him to."

"Still, I do have the guest room in case things change." He knelt in front of her and took her hand into his. "I'd hate to think I've created issues for you with your parents. Maybe if I talk to your mother—"

"It's not you. The problems have been there since I gave up my accounting firm and became Gabriella and Sophia's nanny. She thinks I should have just gotten married and had babies of my own. Now moving across the country to help you just upsets her further. Though none of it has to do with you, she just wants me to settle down, to be barefoot and pregnant in the kitchen like she was." She kept her gaze on the floor and prepared to bare her soul.

"My parents were hard workers, but we didn't have much, even with Dad working two jobs and Mom working part-time while we were in school. We lived in a small two-bedroom house. My parents gave me and Sam the master bedroom since we had to share it. The point is, she always expected me to follow in her footsteps, marry young and have babies before I turned twenty-one. She didn't support me going to college but assumed I'd meet a man to marry there so she didn't fuss much. When I didn't, she told me I should join an accounting firm a town over because of the young males who worked there, but instead I started my own business. Now she sees this as my final shove off, and that she'll never see me living the life she wants for me."

"What about Sam?"

"He's always been supportive of me living my own life, and like I said, we're close. He works on an offshore oil rig that keeps him busy. When he's home—only once every three weeks for a week off—he still lives with our parents and tries to keep thing peaceful between everyone. He would never come here because it would ruffle feathers, especially with Mom."

"*Amore*, I'm sorry."

Words stuck in her throat and she did the only thing she could, she nodded. Her family wasn't the best and they had their faults, but they were hers. She loved them even through the hurt they were causing her now. She could only hope that one day, her mother, who was the cause of the tension, saw what she was doing and eased back.

Then she could live her life on her own terms without having to defend every move she made.

Life would be so much easier if Mom would just accept my choices. Gabriella and Sophia are my daughters, I'm not giving them up just because I didn't give birth to them.

Chapter Eleven

The girls lay on their backs, little chubby arms swatting at the toys that dangled from the play sets in front of the fireplace at Mac's parents' home, just as he had as a child while the adults sat chatting. Mac had his arm around Nicole's shoulder, her body pressed close against him, while his parents sat across from them. He had expected tension as Nicole meshed with his parents, but things were easy as if she had always been a part of the family.

His mother already pulled him aside to express her joy of Mac's choice. If he was honest with himself, he had to admit he was surprised she made no comment about the obvious age different, and he didn't mention it. Instead, if she had her way, she'd have them married by the end of the month. No matter how he denied things weren't at that level, his mother still insisted, *you will be, my son, she's the one for you.* He wanted to believe her, but the logical side of him warned he should brace for the battles ahead.

Even his brother had given his approval, but not before he got in a few remarks about robbing the cradle. At least Angelo hadn't said it in front of his parents or Nicole. His little brother never thought he'd see the day when Mac settled down, so much he had to pull up the news channel on his phone to check and make sure Hell hadn't frozen over yet. *Smart ass.*

Too bad Angelo had to take off early to prepare for a big case. As a Marine Corps JAG officer, there was always something to keep him on his toes. His mother's voice pulled him back from the thoughts of his brother.

"Nicole, if you ever need help with the girls and Mac isn't available you just call me. I'd gladly help with these bundles of joy, anytime."

"Thank you, Mrs. García."

"Now what did I tell you?" His mother set her coffee mug aside and gave Nicole a pointed look.

"I'm sorry, Maria." Nicole smiled, blushing.

"Mom, that reminds me, could you and Dad come over and watch the girls the day after tomorrow? I wanted to take Nicole out to do some Christmas shopping, and get some additional things for the girls."

"I'd love to."

"I'll come too, give your mom a hand and see about doing some work on the house." His father stood. "Ladies, if you'll excuse Mac and me for a moment, I'd like to show him the cabinet I've restored for his guest bathroom."

Mac had a feeling his father would try to get him alone just like his mother had. He pressed his lips to Nicole's temple. "You okay?"

"I'm fine, but shouldn't we be leaving? The girls have to get to bed soon."

"Ten minutes and you'll have him back," Tony promised.

Mac followed his father through the house and out the back door to the workshop, with hopes that whatever he was about to hear would be along the lines of what his mother already stated. He wanted both of his parents to like Nicole because even if things didn't work out romantically, she would always be a big part of his life. They shared children together now.

"What do you think?" Dad nodded toward the antique cabinet that had been original to the house. When they brought it over, Mac had little hope it would survive, but there it was looking as good as ever. The wood was smooth and stained to a warm brown, the polished handles decorated the front. There was a circular cut in the top for where the sink would go, now that they had repurposed it.

"I never thought you'd be able to save it. It was so rough."

"I have a way of bringing life to the unwanted."

Mac glanced back at his dad. "I know, I'm a prime example," he joked, knowing he'd get a kick out of it. His parents had never hidden the fact he was adopted, instead they reminded him all the time they chose him, unlike all the other parents who got saddled with their brats, as his father always joked. They had even embraced his decision to seek out his birth mother, one that in the end only led to a gravestone.

"Yes, and now you're doing the same."

"Gabriella and Sophia aren't unwanted, they're orphans." For some unknown reason he felt the need to defend them; Shawn hadn't left them like his biological parents had.

"True, but you're still willing to step up and give them the family they deserve. That's the man we raised you to be and we couldn't be prouder of you." He leaned against the workbench. "Now this Nicole, she seems like a very nice woman."

"But?" Mac prompted when his father stopped. He only hoped the age difference wasn't about to rear its ugly head.

"She seems very committed to the girls, which is good, and your mother said you're planning to have the paperwork drawn up to share custody. If you screw things up with her, you could lose Gabriella and Sophia. Are you prepared for that?"

"I'm not going to screw this up. Nicole and I have something I've never felt with another woman, there's a bond there. But more than that it's chemistry, like we're made for each other."

"It's the same with your mother and me." Tony grabbed a rag from the bench and started to rub his hand with it, as if he was trying to clean off some invisible dirt. "This brings me to my next point, one I know you're not going to like very much. Maybe it's time you considered retirement. You've put in more than anyone could ask for, you've done your twenty years. Consider staying here with your new family, with all of us."

"Dad..." Mac leaned against the cabinet, the air suddenly gone from his lungs. Of all the things he considered hearing from his father, retirement wasn't one of them. They had always supported his career.

"I just want you think of how Nicole feels. The girls have already lost two parents, should you risk yourself after all of this?"

Mac was unsure if he should be angry or not. Being a SEAL was his life, the very idea of retiring made him sick. How could he do anything but what he'd done his whole life? He wasn't worried about the money, he could always sell the house if he needed to. He was worried about what he'd become without the thrill and adrenaline. Would he still be the same man?

It was inevitable that someday the time would come that he'd have to retire. His body wouldn't keep up with the demands forever. Until a few days ago, he had hoped he'd die in battle. To go down in a blaze of glory surrounded by the brass casings of used rounds and his men would be the best way for him to leave his world.

Otherwise, he might go stir crazy with boredom.

With Gabriella and Sophia changed and put down for the night, Nicole stepped out onto the porch. Mac had taken refuge there while she slipped out of her dress and into gray yoga pants and a matching long sleeve shirt. He had been distant since he returned from the shed with his father, making her wondering what had happened between the two of them. Did it have something to do with her? She thought Maria and Tony had liked her, that the evening had gone smoothly. Maybe it was just a show so as not to cause tension. Whatever it was, she was about to get to the bottom of it.

"Mac?" He had been so lost in his thoughts she wasn't sure he heard the door open and shut. To be safe, she called to him as she came up behind him, because in the time they had been together she learned he didn't like being snuck up on. It tensed every muscle in his body, putting him on edge, ready to attack.

She laid her hand on the railing and watched him. His body was relaxed so he knew she was there but he didn't turn to look at her or say anything. He just gazed out at the darkness and remained silent. Whatever was on his mind had him stressed. Was it work? Would he be deployed before they had time to celebrate Christmas? Or worse yet, before they had time to draw up the paperwork for the girls? If something happened to him while he was deployed, what would happen to the twins, would she lose them? Her mind was brimming with questions until she forced herself to take a deep breath and calm down. This was no time to have a panic attack. Right now Mac needed her.

Her fingers itched to be drawn through his short, thick blond hair, to watch the glints of silver around his temples peak through like diamonds in the sky. Damn he was gorgeous, even when he was a million miles away mentally. She wanted him like she had never wanted anyone before.

There was a soft side he kept hidden from everyone else; the world saw he wasn't a man to be fucked with. When she first met him, she realized she needed to tread carefully with him, especially when it came to custody of the girls. She suspected his *don't fuck with me attitude* was from all his years as a SEAL, but tonight when she met his brother she realized it was a family trait. Angelo had the same attitude and protection mentality that Mac had. His eyes held a haunted look like he'd seen the worst in people and it had begun to make him jaded.

Both the García brothers needed a woman's touch to show them there was still good in life. She was just the woman to do that for Mac, and hopefully Angelo would find someone to help ease the pain she'd seen in his eyes. Angelo worked too hard, it showed in his salt and pepper hair. At thirty-five, he had far more gray than Mac who was nearly five years older.

"Go back inside. You'll catch a chill."

Mac's order brought her back into the moment. "Come with me."

"I'll be in soon."

She put her hand on his back. "What's going on with you? Since coming back from your parents' house, you've been more distant than when you found out I was twenty-four. What's going on in that head of yours? Do your parents not approve?"

"It has nothing to do with us. My parents love you and the girls."

"Then you admit there's something bothering you. Why can't you talk to me? Mac, please, look at me and tell me what's going on." When he didn't, she pulled her hand away as if she'd been burned and stepped back. She wasn't going to stand there in the cold when he insisted on remaining closed off. These moments when he withdrew deep inside himself were becoming irritating. They were still getting to know each other and every time he shut her out, it set them back. "Fine, goodnight then."

"Wait." He reached out, grabbed hold of her wrist, and pulled her into his embrace. "I'm sorry, *amore*, I was just thinking."

"You can talk to me."

"Let's go inside." He held her for a moment longer before finally letting his embrace drop away as he slipped his hand into hers. "Talking to someone is new to me. I've always been distance when there's something I need to figure out, but I guess if you're going to be in this for the long haul you have a right to voice your opinions."

"Why does that very comment send uncertainties rushing through my mind?"

"*Amore*, that's because you are a worrier, where I'm the planner and will work us out of any situation we find ourselves in. So have no qualms." He opened the door and the heat from the house welcomed them. "I could start a fire."

"I believe you're stalling." She raised her eyebrow, waiting for him to spill whatever had prompted his silence. "Let's sit down and you can tell me what's on your mind." With her hand in his, she strolled through the entryway and into the living room toward the sofa. "Now out with it."

"So demanding." He smirked and pulled her onto his lap, surprising her. But she didn't pull away. "The cabinet Dad refinished is beautiful. It will take the place of the counter in the downstairs bathroom. He's got the hole cut out for the sink already and—"

Biting back a sigh, she interrupted him. "This isn't what I meant, but we can take the long way around to you telling me what's gotten you worked up. Though I'll warn you, now that the girls have returned to sleeping through the night, I had considered other adventures for this evening."

"Now that sounds promising." He ran his hand up her thigh, slipping under the edge of the long sleeve shirt.

"Not until you confide in me." She pressed her hand over his, stopping his movements.

"Dad thinks I should retire. Twins are twice as demanding, so it's time to settle down and be a proper family man."

Not wanting him to jump to any conclusion, she stilled. "What do you want?"

"I was just about to ask you that, after all you'd be the one stuck with the girls if I'm deployed. You'd be alone, without any help, since you are against me hiring a nanny." He reminded her of the earlier conversation and let his head fall back against the edge of the sofa.

"I can handle the girls. If I need help, we can get a nanny, or there are always your parents and occasionally babysitters. Don't worry about that, you need to do what's right for you, what you actually want."

He lifted his head back up until their gazes met. "What about you? It's not just about me anymore. I need to consider you, Gabriella, and Sophia."

"Mac, if it was about your career I wouldn't have come to Virginia. I would have fought you for the girls and kept them in Texas. I wouldn't have agreed to this, and I wouldn't be here with you now, opening up my heart to you. I would never ask you to be other than what you are, and your career adds to who you are. If you want to retire then do it, if you want to continue know that I'll support you."

To some, it might have been empty words, but to her it wasn't. His career was important to him and she understood that. Hell, she respected it. What he did was an amazing thing. There would be times when he was gone more than he was home, there would be stress and uphill battles, but she realized she was in this for the long haul. It might have started out for the girls, but she was falling in love with him. It scared her that it was happening so quickly, and it made her want to put her heels in the sand, but it was also empowering. She never knew love could make her feel so free.

"Thank you." He leaned forward and claimed her lips for the first time. It was tender at first, just a light peck, but she leaned into him and it grew deeper as he sucked her bottom lip into his mouth before letting it go again. She released a soft moan as he slid his tongue into her mouth. Then he pressed one last kiss on her lips before pulling back.

Damn, that man is good.

Before she could gather her thoughts, he dove back into the conversation. "I don't want to give it up. Retirement wouldn't suit me; I'm not one to do nothing. I know you and the girls would keep me busy, but I need the rush I get from my job."

"You don't need to defend your decision to me. I know everything will work out fine. When you're home we'll make the moments count. I only ask one thing."

"If it's joint custody of the twins, you have it. I'll calling Mr. Batty tomorrow to have him draw up the paperwork right away. I don't want to take the chance that I could be called up on a mission before the paperwork is signed."

She shook her head. "It's not that. I want you to promise me you'll do everything in your power to come home to us." Swallowing her tears, she watched how his eyes glaze over as if he was thinking about the men he'd lost, the men who would never make it back home to their families.

"I will, *amore*, I will."

Chapter Twelve

The last few days had flown by, leaving just over a week until Christmas, and there was still so much Mac wanted to get done. They had only been in Virginia a short time but Nicole and the twins had settled in comfortably and everything was going smoothly. Even their shopping expedition had gone over without a hitch, and he despised shopping. Thanks to his parents, it was a day they were able to spend completely alone together, and it gave them time to get to know each other better. He had tried to take things slow, but he wasn't sure how much longer he could hold off his desires to have her in the most intimate way possible.

He pulled the last box of Christmas decorations from one of the guest bedroom closets where he had stored it and glanced out the window for the hundredth time. The package from Mr. Batty with the custody papers and Nicole's Christmas gift had been overnighted, now all he had to do was wait for them. Instead of stalking the mailman, he decided to gather the Christmas ornaments, so that evening they could decorate the tree. This year he had decided on a real Christmas tree, one he had gone out hours before to cut down himself. It would be the first real tree since he had lived with his parents. Most years he had been too busy to consider decorating and last year his team volunteered for a mission around the holidays, so they hadn't even been home.

This Christmas was going to be the first memorable one since he was a child. He'd make it special for his new family. The girls wouldn't remember it but they'd have a picture album to look back on, and even if they didn't it was something he and Nicole would always cherish. Their first Christmas together, the four of them. *Look at me, I'm turning into a family man.*

Tires crunching on the gravel driveway had him setting the box aside and going back to the window just in time to see Angelo's truck making its way toward the house. What could he want at this time of the day? He should be in his office preparing or in court prosecuting the next big case. Angelo didn't have the highest conviction rate in the JAG core without putting in endless hours. It was unlike him to leave his office while there was still sunlight.

With only one way to find out, he turned and headed downstairs to the front door. He stepped into the hallway just as Nicole came out of the nursery with Gabriella and Sophia on each hip. "Someone's coming up the drive, are you expecting anyone?"

"It's Angelo." As she neared her, he reached over and plucked Sophia from Nicole's arms. "How's my sweet pea?"

"It seems when you're around no one wants me." Nicole bounced Gabriella up on her hip and shook her head at the girls. "Somehow I went from being their whole world, to second place."

"You want Mommy, too, don't you?" He glanced down at Sophia, who only giggled in response. "See I told you. Does the fact that *I* want you make up for it?" He slid his hand up her arm, teasing his finger along the lines of her freckles.

"Maybe you'll have to show me just how much you want me," she teased.

A truck door shut, reminding him time was short before Angelo would be ringing the doorbell. "Soon, *amore*, soon." Not having time to show her just how much how he wanted her, he headed downstairs. He had been waiting to take things further but was respecting that she might need time. Everything in her life had changed so quickly he didn't want to rush her.

"Mac…" The concern in her voice made him pause halfway down the steps and turn back to her. "As much as I like the sound of Mommy, are you sure it's the best idea?"

"We agreed we'd raise the girls as our own. Mommy, Daddy, that's who we are to them. When they're older we'll tell them about their parents, but for now this is the best way. Our little girls are blessed with two sets of parents, one watching over them and us." The doorbell rang and he was forced to put his worries for their future aside. He bounced Sophia on his hip. "Let's find out what my brother wants."

"Mac, I know you're in there. Open up." Angelo yelled through the closed door.

"Wait." On the last step, Nicole stopped him with a brief touch on his shoulder. "Give me Sophia and I'll take the girls back upstairs. You might need to be alone."

"I doubt it's anything like that but whatever he's here for can be said in front of you. Remember, no secrets. We're a team now, we face any issue together." Keeping Sophia in his arms, Mac pulled open the door. "I was just checking to see if Hell had frozen over, you never leave work at this time of day."

"Which one are you, little one?" Angelo asked the baby in Mac's arms as if he thought she'd answer.

"Sophia." Mac tipped his head. "Gabriella is over there."

"How do you keep them straight?"

"Sophia's hair in two shades lighter than Gabriella's and her temperament is a little different. She's more easy-going and is the snuggle bug of the two." Nicole came to stand next to Mac. "She's also a little smaller in size."

"Women notice those things. Men would need shirts to tell them apart." Angelo pulled his finger back from Sophia. "Are you going to invite me in? Or leave us all stand in the cold until we're sick? That's fine with me but I don't think you want two sick babies on your hands with the holidays."

"Come in." Mac stepped back allowing his brother to enter, then shut the door and strolled toward the living room.

"Can I get you some coffee or anything, Angelo?"

"No thank you." He smiled at Nicole. "I've got to be back in court shortly, so I only have a few minutes."

"Are you going to tell me what brings you here or shall I start guessing?" He sat Sophia down in the playpen.

"Can we have a minute alone?"

"Just…" Mac started to tell Angelo just to tell him whatever it was but Nicole cut him off.

"Go ahead, I've got the girls." She sat Gabriella down next to Sophia and looked between the men. "It's fine."

Mac caught Nicole's hand and tipped his head toward the library. "I'll be just down the hall."

"It's only going to take a minute," Angelo said from behind them.

Mac shared one last took with Nicole before forcing himself to step away and stroll down the hallway. Inside the library, he shoved his hands into the pockets of his jeans and waited. Whatever Angelo wanted to talk to him about alone had better be important, because in that moment he had just wanted to be with Nicole and the girls. They were supposed to be spending the day getting the house ready for Christmas and enjoying the normalcy of life when he wasn't on Navy duty.

Angelo shut the door behind him and cut to the chase. "I spoke with Dad this morning. He mentioned he suggested you retire."

"If you're here to try to convince me to retire, you're wasting your time."

"Actually I'm here to tell you to think twice before you jump into a decision. The military is something we've wanted our whole lives. Could you see yourself living the dull life that others lead, leaving behind the excitement? This isn't something you can change your mind about once the paperwork is started. You know our parents have always wanted us to be happy and have supported our careers. You've just thrown Dad for a loop, making him a granddad without any warning."

Mac rolled his shoulders and tried to force the tension away. "I've already spoken to Nicole about it, I'm not retiring."

"Nicole? How serious are things between you two?"

"Serious enough that she has a say." Mac had always been superstitious and didn't want to say she was the one he'd been waiting for all these years, but it was what he was thinking.

"Seems like things are progressing between you two rather quickly. Have you thought this through?"

"I have. She's not one of those flag-chasing women who hang around the bars military personnel frequent. Nicole is unlike any woman I've met, and we're going to raise the twins together." *More than that if I have my say.*

"Mom might be right. She said you had fallen for Nicole, but I didn't believe her. I didn't think a woman could ever tame my big brother." Angelo let out a light laugh.

"Tame…not the word I would have used, but whatever it is, it isn't so bad. Maybe you should consider it. You know there's more to life than just the next big case." As the words left Mac's lips he wondered when he'd started thinking about more than just the latest mission. *When Nicole entered my life, that's when.*

"They've already been telling me it's time for me to think of the same thing. That I could have a successful legal practice outside of the military, that I need to find a wife of my own." With a distant look in his eyes, Angelo slipped his hand into the pocket of his Marine dress uniform. "Can you really see a woman settling for a workaholic like me?"

"You'd be surprised. Look at Nicole."

"Women like her are hard to come by, especially in your line of work." Angelo's shoulders slumped just enough to make Mac wonder if his brother had been searching for a serious relationship.

Even though Mac had been adopted, while Angelo had been born to their parents a few years later, they were still two peas from the same pod. They were close, sharing the same goals and dreams most of their lives. Even now, he could see Angelo wanted what he had, he wanted a woman he could come home to when the days were done. What their mother called the big old Italian heart. They were protective of women, even strangers, and they both wanted to stand up for what was right.

"I've got to get back to the base. I'll see you at Mom and Dad's for Christmas dinner, right? I have plans to mark my nieces so I can tell them apart." Angelo broke the silence that had settled over them.

"Nothing permanent," Mac warned, then nodded. "We'll be there. Nicole and I have decided to incorporate traditions into the Christmas celebration for the girls. Just like we always went out with Dad to cut down our own Christmas tree, we're going to do that once the girls are older. Christmas dinner with everyone is one we're not going to lose, though Nicole mentioned doing it here next year to take some of the burden off Mom, but we'll see what the year brings."

"Good, then I'll see everyone on Christmas."

This was the first Christmas since Mac was a boy that he was actually looking forward to Christmas. For the first time in a long time, there seemed to be something to celebrate. He had two beautiful daughters and a woman he wanted in his life for years to come. Everything was perfect.

While the girls played in their playpen, Nicole sat with a book opened in her lap. Because her mind was wandering, she hadn't actually read any of it. Her thoughts kept going over the same things and every time she thought something was taken care of she started doubting it. Never in her life had she waffled back and forth as much as she was doing now over having the girls call her Mom. She wanted it more than she had ever expected, but there was a part of her that wondered if she wasn't doing a disservice to the woman who had actually given birth to them, and more importantly to Shawn. Would the girls one day understand why they had raised them as their own children?

It seemed almost crazy to doubt such a minor thing, especially since people did it all the time. The girls deserved real parents and they could be that for them. It was what Shawn would have wanted, so why did she doubt it?

As if lightning had struck, she realized she wasn't doubting the word *mom*, but what it would mean for her relationship with Mac. It brought their connection to another level. Going down the path that led her to him, she had to be serious about it or shit would hit the fan and quickly. She had been truthful when she said his career didn't bother her; it was dangerous but what he did was honorable. If their love was strong enough it would overcome any separation the military threw at them.

What she wasn't sure she could get past was his family. They seemed nice enough, but having grown up in a home with two hardworking parents, she never had family surrounding her. It would be different having them pop in whenever they felt like it, just as Angelo had done today. Or having the grandparents part of the girls' life, possibly daily. Growing up, she'd always wanted a big family, and now here was her chance. The girls could grow up surrounded by a group of people who loved them and maybe a house full of siblings.

"Nicole, I'm leaving, but I'll see you at Christmas dinner." Angelo paused just inside the doorway. "Don't let my brother get out of hand, keep him in place."

"Don't worry, he's behaving himself." *Too much actually.* Angelo paused as if he wanted to say something else before he finally gave her a nod, turned on his heels, and headed for the door. Mac came in a few minutes later and sat next to her. "That was a quick visit."

"He spoke with Dad this morning and wanted to let me know how he felt about me retiring." He plucked the book off her lap and lifted her into his arms.

"Are you receiving pressure from him?"

"Actually, no, he just wanted to make sure I thought about it before I submitted my request for retirement. I told him we've already made up our minds and I'd be telling Dad soon enough. Now what about this Christmas tree, are you ready to decorate it?"

Before she could answer it, the doorbell rang again. Her heart skipped a beat with the hope that this was the delivery they had been expecting. The final custody papers for the girls, granting her shared custody. The very thing she wanted since Shawn had died now made her nervous. Legally she would be the twins' mother, and was responsible for them. *What am I doing? I can't even keep a plant alive.*

"I'll get that, then we're going to go out to celebrate. There's a little Italian place just off the boardwalk that's delicious." With a quick kiss to her forehead he stood up, taking her with him. "The day we officially become parents seems like something we should celebrate. Now go get ready. I've got the girls."

"I thought we were going to decorate?"

"We will tonight." He hollered over his shoulder. "An early dinner, and tonight we'll have this place ready for Christmas."

Why did the idea of dinner with him seem so intimate? It wasn't like they'd be alone, Gabriella and Sophia would be with them, but it almost seemed like a date. Gabriella's coos from the crib had her glancing in that direction, only to find her little fists power-punching the air. Almost as if to say: *Go, Mommy!*

Chapter Thirteen

Mac laid the custody papers on the coffee table and held the small rectangular white box with the bright red ribbon in his hands. "Your mommy is going to love this. Now be quiet while I go hide this." He glanced at them one last time before he dashed down the hall toward the den. For now, he'd hide it in his tools; she had no reason to go there, and he'd only have to keep it hidden from her for a few days until Christmas.

With the task complete, he tugged his cell phone out of his pocket, slid his finger over the contacts until he found his parents' number, and brought it to his ear. After two rings, his mother answered.

"Mac, we were just talking about you. Would you guys like to come over for dinner tonight?"

"Actually, Mom, I know it's last minute but would you be able to watch Gabriella and Sophia? We've received the custody papers and I wanted to take Nicole out to celebrate our parenthood." He heard the girls giggling as he headed back to the living room. They might not understand what was going on but seemed to be as excited as he was about the delivery.

"Sure. What time do you need us there?"

"Nicole's getting ready now, so whenever you can get here." He looked over at the steps. "I thought an early dinner, then a stroll along the boardwalk, but we'll be home early since we had plans to decorate the house tonight."

"I'm baking cookies for the cookie exchange but if you don't mind me bringing it along so I can use your kitchen, then we'll be there in fifteen minutes." In the background, he could hear his mother's mixer.

"You're always welcome in my kitchen at the cost of you leaving a few chocolate chip cookies."

"Deal." The mixer shut off. "We'll be there shortly and I'm glad you're going to have a quiet dinner, just the two of you. You need nights like this, it's a key thing in relationships."

"Thanks, Mom." He pulled the phone away from his ear, slid his finger over the screen to end the call, and squatted in front of the playpen. "You're going to be good for Grammy, right, my beautiful Gabriella and Sophia?"

"What's this about Grammy?" Nicole's heels clicked against the hardwood as she came down the steps.

"I've called Mom, she's going to come over and watch the girls while we go out."

"That wasn't necessary."

"I know. I thought it would be nice for us to have some quality time alone. I guess you could call it our first real date. If you're worried about her looking after the girls I can call her and cancel."

She shook her head, sending a strand of brown hair falling from the clip she'd tied it back in. "No, it's fine. She raised two amazing sons. I have confidence she can look after the girls for a few hours."

"Good." He rose from where he knelt. "I'll change then, and Mom should be here in fifteen minutes."

"My beautiful girls, you know we'll be back in a bit and I want you to be very good." She lifted Gabriella from the playpen, tossing her lightly in the air before kissing her plump cheeks.

"I love seeing you with the girls, it's beautiful. You are a natural mother and hopefully you can help my parenting nature come out."

"You're a good father. This makes us a good team and a hell of a lot better than some parents. Now get dressed and we'll have a little quiet time to get to know each other better."

He hurried upstairs, not bothering to hide his excitement about their evening together. *Tonight I'm going to make you mine in every way possible.*

It was later than they had expected when Nicole and Mac arrived back at the house, so late Maria had already fed and put the girls to bed. It had been a wonderful evening and coming home to find everything done for them made it even better. She stood by the window while Mac saw his parents out, her thoughts returning to their walk along the beach. It had been the first time she had seen the beach and it was beautiful. The sounds of the waves crashing on the shore still reverberated in her mind, and a bit of sand remained between her toes. It was the closest anyone could get to Heaven while still alive.

"*Amore,* you look a million miles away." Mac placed his hand on the small of her back.

"I've been thinking about the beach. I can't wait until the girls are older and we can take them there and let them play in the surf." She let her head fall back against his shoulder. "Since your dad put the Christmas tree in the stand and gave it water, would you be upset if we waited to do the decorating until tomorrow?"

"No, *amore,* I had different plans for this evening anyway."

She tipped her head back enough to look at him. "What is that?"

"I want you to wait here, I just need five minutes."

"You're on the clock." She teased as he stepped away from her and headed for the steps.

She didn't know what he had planned, but if it was anything like the day she had no doubt it would be amazing. He was more considerate than anyone she had known before, going out of his way to please her. It was so romantic to have someone like him interested in her wants and needs. Even with the knowledge of what was ahead of them, it didn't stop him from being romantic, to court her, to get to know her.

She turned away from the window, her gaze traveled around the room before stopping at the Christmas tree. It was only days before Christmas, and instead of grieving for Shawn, she was diving into a relationship with Mac. Hopefully, it would work out for them and the girls. She picked up one of the pink baby blankets and brought it to her nose. All she wanted to give them was a happy, steady home. One that Shawn would have been proud of.

"*Amore.*" Mac called from the top of the steps, keeping his voice low so as not to wake the girls. "You can come up now."

Quickly she folded the blanket, laid it on the back of a chair, and headed for the stairs. Curiosity got the best of her, and she found herself speeding her pace. At the top of the stairs rose petals laid scattered in a trail toward Mac's bedroom where only a flickering soft glow, like that of candles, reflected.

He stood in the doorway, waiting and watching. "This is your chance to slip into your room if you need more time. I won't hold it against you. Or...come to me, and I'll make it a night you'll never forget."

Not wanting to take the chance the click from her heels might stir the girls, she kicked them off and padded barefoot toward him. "I want this, I want you." She stopped just short of touching him.

He reached out and grabbed the sash around her waist that clinched the dress together, showing off a little more curve to her hips than she preferred.

"*Bella.*" *Beautiful.* She wasn't sure she heard him right until he said it again, but this time in English. "My beautiful *amore.* Come, let me take that doubt from your eyes." Stepping backward he pulled her toward the bed by the sash, never breaking eye contact.

As they made their way across the room to the king size bed, she had a brief moment to take into consideration the thought he had put into this night. The candles spread out around the room were the only light, and cast a romantic glow throughout. The rose petals from the hallway continued to the bed, with a few spread out over the blue and white comforter. There was even a fire crackling on the far wall by a small sitting area. It was more romantic than she could have possibly imagined.

They came to stand in front of the bed, the rose petals tickling the bottom of her feet. He leaned into her, pressing his lips to hers, not allowing her a chance to deny him. He tasted of chocolate and powdered sugar from the dessert they had shared over dinner, making her crave more of him.

If Shawn's death taught her anything, it was that she had to live for the moment. She tossed her self-doubts and fears behind her and returned his kisses without hesitation. Having finally come together, things would never be the same for them. It could only get better in the coming days or weeks. With each kiss, she embraced the family and life that was before her, waiting for her to claim it.

He pulled back enough to break the kiss, his mouth still hovering over hers. "I've wanted you since I saw you standing in the doorway with that gun pointed at me. Feisty. Part of me knew in time you'd be mine."

"I'd say the SEALs have made you cocky, but after meeting Angelo I think it might be a family trait."

"A little of both I'm sure." He reached behind her and slid the zipper down her back. With the zipper down, he found the collar of the dress and slowly slid it down her arms, baring her skin inch by inch until she stood there in nothing but her bra and panties. Under the scrutiny of his gaze, she wanted to cover herself, to hide the few extra pounds and the natural curve to her body.

"Don't you dare." He caught her hands before she could wrap them around the front of her body. In one smooth motion he lifted her into his arms and gently laid her on the center of the mattress. "I don't want to see you try to cover up one inch of your beautiful body."

Every time he called her beautiful her heart skipped a beat. All her life she wanted someone to find her attractive for who she was, not wanting someone to try to change her. She wasn't a perfect woman to some men, not with her curves, but overall she was happy with who she was. Whenever anyone had criticized her body, she always told herself she was a sweet sixteen.

"*Amore*, come back to me." He sat beside her, his fingers in her hair. "What were you thinking about that had your mind wandering away from this moment? Doubts, *bella*?"

She shook her head. "I was thinking about the idea of you finding me beautiful. You must have women falling at your feet, but here you are with me and I'm nothing special."

"You're special to me." He leaned into her neck; his teeth grazed the skin by her collarbone. "You're the only woman I want. *Sempre*."

"*Sempre*?"

"It means always in Italian." When she caught hold of a button on his dress shirt and began to undo it, he laid his hand over hers and stopped her. "I don't think that's a good idea."

"Why not?"

"The last time—"

"I looked away, not because of what I saw but because I wanted to touch you. To draw my fingers over the lines of your abs, to feel your tight muscles. It had nothing to do with the scars." She reached up and cupped the side of his face. "We all have scars. Some are hidden while others brand our skin."

"I don't want to see the look in your eyes when you see them. I want this to be a memorable night, not one that has to do with the memories of how I got each one."

"Take off your shirt and let me show you they don't bother me. We all have something we'd rather hide. For me it's the plump figure, for you it's scars, but between us we will hide nothing." His hand loosened over hers and she began undoing the button again. "Tonight is about overcoming our hesitations and coming together in every way."

Her fingers flew over the buttons, quickly undoing each one. In her mind the quicker she got him out of the shirt the sooner he'd see there was nothing to worry about. It would be like pulling a bandage off in one quick motion instead of inch by inch, drawing out the pain. With the shirt open she slid her hands up his chest, the toned muscles warm under her touch. She ran her fingers up his body until his heartbeat fluttered under her touch.

"What do you see in my eyes?"

In answer, he reclaimed her lips as she slid his shirt away. She brushed her fingers over more scars that decorated his back. Not wanting to give him any reason to stop, she let her fingers glide over them until she reached the top of his jeans.

He kissed her neck, nibbling down her jawline to her shoulder. She unbuckled his belt, slid it out of the loops, and tossed it to the floor where it landed with a thump. She let him have a few more minutes of exploration, since he'd finally made it to her breasts. His fingers slipped beneath the thin fabric of her bra, then he teased over the nipple and pushed the bra aside.

She lifted up just enough to reach behind her and unhook her bra. Her nipples had always been extra sensitive, the slightest touch bringing her pleasure. He lowered his mouth to her nipple, his gaze locked on her. She moaned in ecstasy when his tongue flicked over one hardened tip. She tugged on his jeans before he could move lower.

"These need to go." She unbuttoned his pants and guided them gently over his hips.

"Always demanding, *amore*." He rose off the bed and slipped the jeans the rest of the way off, as well as the rest of his clothes, until he stood naked before her. The candle light reflecting off his body made him appear even more delectable, and she had to have him. She craved his touch like nothing before.

He came back to the bed and continued where he'd left off, kissing a path down her neck. Sensations collided and threatened to overwhelm her when he teased her nipples. Pushing her gently back onto the bed, his bulky frame hovered above her as he stared down at her, desire burning in his eyes.

He caressed every inch of her body, sending moans of ecstasy from her lips. His touch was incredibly tender, as though trying to memorize every curve with his hands and mouth. Heat soared through her blood, like a fire burning just below her skin, impatient and demanding.

Taking hold of the string bikini panties, he pulled it down her legs in one quick motion. He blazed a hot, wet trail of kisses across her belly and stroked her thighs with his fingertips. With every touch, she arched her hips, demanding more. She couldn't get enough of him. He nudged her legs farther apart, his fingers delved inside her and she met the teasing thrusts. A demanding moan she barely recognized vibrated in her throat. A trail of wicked kisses tingled over her thighs. He moved his hand and replaced it with his mouth. Tiny nips and gentle licks flicked over her sweet spot, nearly driving her over the edge. She dug her fingers into his back, torn between pressing him closer and dragging him up. She wanted all of him.

"Mac." The one simple word held so much desire and need. "I need you."

"Anything for you, *amore*." He spread her legs farther, giving him the access he needed before filling her slowly, inch by inch. Halfway in, he slid out before thrusting back in, filling her completely with his manhood. His strokes brought to life the need that had been kept hidden within her for years.

He increased his pace, driving the force of each pump. The erotic dance amped up her tension, every delicious glide of his shaft inside her seemed to set off another cascade of heat. Their bodies rocked back and forth, tension stretching her tighter as she fought for the release she longed for. Upon that release, she dug her nails into his back, arching her body into his. He continued to pump until her name escaped his lips and his own ecstasy found him. Eternity stretched on until he collapsed beside her.

Cuddled together in a mixture of exhaustion and utter relaxation while their breathing returned to normal, his fingers caressed her side in long, lazy strokes. Their lovemaking had been more amazing than she could have ever dreamed. His gentle caresses and the way he called out her name as he filled her body with himself almost had her climaxing again. It was pure Heaven, but it also had her heart picking up speed as she realized what was happening. From the beginning, she knew this relationship had to be long-term for the sake of the girls, but she didn't expect it to be like this, especially not so soon.

She loved him.

Chapter Fourteen

The day had been beyond what Mac could have imagined. He wanted to stay in bed, his arms around Nicole, holding her tight. He had to deal with the candles. "I'll be right back." He slipped out of bed.

"Leaving me already," she teased.

"No, you're going to stay cuddled next to me until the girls force us to wake up." He blew out each flame, leaving only the glow from the fireplace. All of a sudden, he felt a hand on his back. "*Merda!*" He should have known better than to get out of bed without putting his shirt back on. His back was the worst of his scars.

"So much detail. It's beautiful." She touched the America flag he had tattooed between his shoulder blades. The flag in mid-wave, the words *freedom isn't free* above it. Within the flag were the names of the men he had lost under his command.

"Don't." The word came out softer than he expected. "It's been too long since I've had to worry about someone seeing my scars."

"Why? I showed you they don't bother me."

"These are the worse. The shrapnel…" He turned to face her.

"Mac, stop trying to protect me. I know what your job entails, the danger, and it doesn't change anything. Seeing the scars won't change this. Don't turn from me."

It was in his blood to protect her. His father had drilled it into him from an early age to protect women and children, and the military had only made that instinct stronger. Instead of fighting with her, he wrapped his arms around her waist. "Every time I see them it's a reminder of what put them there. My job is dangerous."

"The *world* is dangerous. Parents can't even send their kids to school without worrying they might not come home at the end of the day. None of us are guaranteed tomorrow. While we're alive and sharing our days together I won't allow you to shut me out." She wrapped her arms around his neck. "I know you don't want to talk about what happened, and I'm not asking you too. Please, don't put up barriers."

"I have a feeling I'm going to have my work cut out with you."

"Then I'll start the first challenge. The names…" She traced her finger over the tattoo.

"Those are the names of the men I failed. I have them there so they'll never be forgotten." He paused for a moment, letting the words sink in before he tipped his head toward the other side of the room. "Now let's go back to bed."

With a yawn, she wiggled her eyebrows. "What did you have in mind?"

"Just to lay there and talk until we fall asleep. The girls might be sleeping through the night but it won't be long before they wake us." Taking her hand in his, he moved them toward the mattress.

"Tomorrow will make five days until Christmas and we still need to decorate. There's still stuff I'd like to get for the girls. I'd like to see about finding the girls some outfits at Wynn's children's boutique. They are growing so fast and they need something for Christmas dinner with your family."

"We can go tomorrow if you'd like." Pulling her into bed next to him, he snuggled against her.

She laid her hand in the crook of his arm, dragging her fingers over the scars on his chest. "All scars tell a story." She traced over the deepest scars. "I doubt you could see it in the faint light but I have one just below my breasts. It's from a knife, and it's smooth unlike these, but when I see it in the mirror…it reminds me. Just as I'm sure yours do. Though mine brought something good from it."

"What happened?"

"My father stabbed me." She paused, touching the scar on her chest. "It's the first time I've said it out loud. I was sixteen and just came home from my first real date. My father had been drinking and was upset the boy tried to give me a goodnight kiss. In anger, my father lashed out. At the time I thought he was trying to hit my date…I didn't see the knife. Not until it was too late. I had moved to stop him when the knife slid home, deep within my body."

"Oh, *amore*."

"It turned out for the best. His drinking started as a way to relax after working two jobs, but it quickly spiraled out of control and he couldn't stop. This accident was the wakeup call he needed to get help. He hasn't touched a drop since that night."

"He could have killed you," Mac reasoned, his voice laced with anger and sadness.

"Too close for comfort, but I lived." She tipped her head to look up at him. "Sam beat the shit out of him and told him either give up the bottle or Sam was going to quit school, find a job, and take Mom and I away. He refused to have us live like that any longer. Before that night, Sam and I weren't very close, probably because we had to share a room for so long. We just got sick of each other. He hated all the times I'd lock him out of the room, or when I'd wake up screaming because I had another dream about spiders, or other creepy bugs. But that night it was different, I could see it in his eyes, he wanted to kill our father for what he had done."

"What about your father?"

"That night he checked himself into rehab. Mom was angry because he wasn't there when she thought I was dying but he did the right thing. I was never sure if it was what he did or Sam's threat that made my father see what he was doing, but it didn't matter."

If Sam hadn't stepped in that night, or threatened his father, who knew what could have happened the next time something angered him?

Thanks to Sam, Mac now had the one woman who held his heart.

Sounds like a damn fine man. I owe him. And I wish there were more like him.

The ring of the doorbell pulled Nicole from a deep sleep. She glanced around the dark room, trying to gather her surroundings, until she caught a glimpse of Mac coming awake beside her and the night returned to her. It hadn't been an amazing dream; it was real.

"*Merda!*"

As her eyes finally focused, she caught sight of the alarm clock. Just after two o'clock in the morning. "Who could that be at this hour?"

"I don't know but I'll kill them if they wake Gabriella and Sophia." He slipped out of bed and grabbed his jeans from the floor. "You stay here while I find out."

Unable to find her own clothes, she grabbed his discarded dress shirt and headed for the hallway. Someone at the door at this hour could only mean one thing. Had something happened to his parents? His brother? Surely if he was being deployed his commanding officer would have called, not showed up at the door. She wasn't sure how it worked but going door to door to gather the troops seemed to be a waste of time.

"Nicole Marie Ryan, open this damn door!" Fists pounded against the door, echoing through the house.

"Sam?" She started down the steps, buttoning the shirt as she went. It was a little tight across her hips and breasts but at least it covered all the important parts. Sam hollered about something she couldn't make out, and she sped her pace. What was he doing here?

Mac opened the door and Sam rushed him, slamming him against the wall. Mac didn't fight back, he just let it happen, and there was no doubt in her mind that if he wanted to stop it he could take her brother down without an issue. Sam might have been in good shape—he built up muscles working on the oil rig—but he wasn't a match for Mac.

"Sam, what the hell are you doing?" She stepped up beside them, placing her hand on his arm. Looking at her brother, she realized he hadn't slept. His eyes were bloodshot, his normally clean-shaven look was replaced with messy stubble, but most of all he looked worn out and stressed.

"Mom called, said you were being brainwashed and held against your will because this bastard needed someone to care for those children. I've come to get you and the girls. No way am I letting this bastard do this to you and Shawn's kids."

"What the hell—"

"Don't lie to me because he's here. Now get your stuff and the girls." Sam glared at her, his eyes filled with rage. "I've only got a short leave from the rig to take care of this. Now move!"

"I think you should listen to your sister," Mac stated, his voice tight from Sam's arm pressed against his neck.

"Whatever she's going to tell me is a lie because you've threatened to take those girls from her. She's been the only mother they know, and she loves them, so what gives you the right to—"

"Stop this, Sam." She squeezed her brother's arm until he looked at her. "Mom is the one lying to you. I came here of my own free will. Now get off him so we can talk and I can prove it to you."

Sam loosened his hold on Mac. "How?"

"Come over here." She stepped away from him and went to the coffee table, scooping up the papers Mr. Batty had sent. "These are papers for Gabriella and Sophia granting me joint custody. Does that sound like he's keeping me here against my will? I could leave here at any time and take the girls but I don't want to. I don't know why Mom lied to you, but he's not brainwashing me."

"How do I know the papers are legit? Maybe he has a friend who whipped them up." Sam let go of Mac and walked to the sofa.

"Mr. Batty sent them this morning." Mac rolled his neck. "You know him, don't you? He's from your town."

She stood there holding the papers out to him. "Look at them for yourself if you don't believe me."

"Why would Mom lie to me?" He leaned against the side of the sofa, appearing hurt and confused. "I could have lost my job. I was preparing to leave without getting the time off approved because I thought you needed me. I failed you before but I swore I wouldn't this time."

"You didn't fail me." She tossed the papers aside and strolled to him, taking his hand.

"That night with Dad, I failed you. Do I need to beat the shit out of this asshole too?"

Smirking toward Mac, she let out a lighthearted chuckle. "That won't be necessary."

Sam looked between Nicole and Mac before returning his attention to her. "I thought you'd say that." He nodded to the shirt she was wearing, Mac's shirt. "So I've come all this way for nothing."

"I wouldn't say nothing. You got to see me, and if you stick around the girls would like to see you when they get up. It's time to introduce them properly to their Uncle Sam."

"What?"

"We've decided to raise the girls as our own, together." Mac came to her and wrapped his arm around her waist. "With Nicole as their mother and me as their father. That makes them your nieces. You're more than welcome to stay here, get some sleep, and we can discuss anything else in the morning. You're family and welcome in my home as long as you respect it. I won't have you upsetting Nicole or the twins with these hateful lies. Is that understood?"

"It seems like I made a bad first impression. I'm Sam Ryan." He held out his hand to Mac.

"Mac García." Mac took his hand, giving it a firm shake before releasing it.

"I know who you are. Mom made a big fuss some Navy SEAL had come and kidnapped her daughter. She wanted to call the cops, but Dad wouldn't let her." He ran his hand through his curly brown hair. "I guess that should have been my first warning something wasn't right. If it had been true, Dad would have been on the phone with the police, FBI, hell even the Admiral."

"*Merda*, I'd have had some serious explaining to do to my CO."

"Mac, I'd like a minute with my brother, could you see that the room next to the nursery is ready?" She tilted her head back to look at him, hoping he didn't mind that she'd stay in his room, giving Sam her bedroom since it was the only finished guest room.

"I'll see you upstairs." Mac leaned down and kissed her lips. It was quick but gave her the reassurance she needed.

She watched Mac leave them and wondered if he realized he didn't have a shirt on. It was nice to see him without his shirt, comfortable and carefree. Maybe it had been the doorbell in the middle of the night that made him forgo it, or it could have been he didn't feel the need to hide them around other men, only her. She wasn't sure and it didn't matter, because whatever the reason it was a step in the right direction.

"If you wanted to tell me how bad I screwed up this time I don't need to hear it."

"No. I wanted…" She stepped away from him and went to sit on the sofa.

"What is it? You've never been one to hold your tongue, so out with it."

"Sam." She wrung her hands in her lap. "I don't know what's happening here."

"You mean between you and Mac? Because it seems pretty clear to me. You're wearing his shirt, which means only one thing."

"Well…yeah." She felt her cheeks burn with embarrassment. This was not something she wanted to talk to her brother about. "What I'm getting at is I don't want you to tell Mom about this. Not yet."

"Embarrassed by your man? That's never a good sign, sis."

"No." She quickly defended herself. "It's not that, far from it. Come on, you know how Mom can be. Look at what she said to get you out here. I want to see where this goes before she knows. Either way, we have to raise the girls together, so I don't need Mom complicating things."

"Mom complicating things…are you sure we're talking about the same person?" Sam teased her and came to sit beside her. "You're secret is safe with me, but you know Mom's not going to lay off. She wants you back home in Texas."

"I know. She wants me back home *without* the girls and to start my accounting practice again." She tucked her hair behind her ear. "It's not what I want."

"Then don't do it. This is your life and I want you happy. I'll stand by you and fight your battles with Mom if you need me to."

"You're the best big brother a girl could ask for." She leaned her head against his shoulder. "I'm sorry Mom made you come all this way for nothing."

"I'd go to the ends of the earth to save you from any heartache." He laid his hand over hers, giving it a gentle squeeze. "Now go to your man. Make sure you tell him your brother isn't always an ass."

"You're never an ass. You were only trying to protect me and for that I love you." Their mother could be overwhelming, and twisted things sometimes to get what she wanted, but Sam was amazing. He wasn't like anyone in the family. He preferred to keep to himself, but when someone was in trouble he'd go to any lengths for them. He had shown it before, and coming to Virginia when he thought she was in trouble he'd shown it again. Now if she could only get her big brother to settle down and off those dangerous oil rigs, everything would be perfect.

 *Chapter Fifteen*

With Gabriella and Sophia in safe hands with Uncle Sam, Nicole and Mac slipped out to do some last minute Christmas shopping. She wasn't sure how she managed to do it but over breakfast she talked Sam into staying until after Christmas. He had the personal leave saved up and for once he agreed to take it. She suspected it had a little to do with returning home to face Mom, but she didn't care, it was still nice to have him there.

"Your thoughts keep you busy, *amore.*" Mac slipped his arm around her waist as they strolled down the boardwalk toward Heart of a Diamond.

"I was thinking about my mother and this latest stunt. My phone call to her this morning seemed to have calmed things to a point, but she's still determined I need to return to Texas. What will she pull next?"

"I've got until after the New Year before my team has to report back for duty. We could take a trip back to Texas and smooth things over with your parents. Let them know I haven't kidnapped their little girl. It might help."

"Or it could make things a million times worse." She glanced out at the water. With the cold breeze off the water and the frigid, rainy weather the beach was deserted and peaceful.

"Give it some thought. We could fly back when Sam goes home and you'd have his support as well as mine when you see them." They walked in silence as she wondered how she could smooth things over with her mother. When they arrived, he held open the door to the boutique for her. "After you, *amore*."

"Mac, Nicole, how nice to see you." Wynn stepped out from behind the counter, her hand on her swollen stomach. "What can I do for you today?"

"We've come to purchase some addition things for the girls." Nicole tried not to stare at Wynn's stomach, but the sight of the pregnant woman made her wonder if someday she would have the same experience. Gabriella and Sophia were her daughters even if she hadn't given birth to them, but she wanted to experience the miracle of having a child grow within her. Would Mac want more children?

"I know I'm huge, and I'm not even due until June." Wynn laughed, rubbing her stomach as if it were a magic lamp. "Why don't you two have a look around, while I step into the back for a moment? I have a couple things that might suit your beautiful girls. Is there anything you're looking for in particular?"

"Christmas dresses for dinner with Mac's family. Other than that just some everyday clothes. They are growing so fast, most of what I have doesn't fit anymore." Nicole took in the boutique, the décor that made it feel posh and festive. She'd never seen such beautiful clothes.

Instantly she was drawn to a cute line of sailor dresses. The white one with the blue collar and flag buttons was adorable. "Do people still stick by the rule of no white after Labor Day?"

"You're seriously asking me?" He raised an eyebrow at her. "I can only tell you that it still applies for the Navy. Our dress whites are only worn in the summer, any other time it's our dress blues. As for fashion, you'd have to ask Wynn. You could always buy a bigger size, or try this." He held up a similar dress but in blue with a red collar.

"I see you've found the military inspired items." Wynn came toward them, carrying a stack of outfits.

"I was just asking Mac if people still stuck with the rule of no white after Labor Day."

"I'm old fashion and say yes, but I know there are people who will wear white any time of the year. Though if you like the outfit I can make sure you get one when it's in season in whatever sizes you need."

"That would be wonderful." Nicole hung the white dress back on the rack and picked out two of the blue ones in the size she needed before turning back to Wynn. "So what did you bring out to show me?"

"Come over here." Wynn walked toward a small counter just to the right of the register. "Since we're just days before Christmas most of the dresses have sold out already. However, I thought you'd like this one."

Wynn held up a black velvet dress that had a sparkly, silver sheer tied around the waist, with the same material around the bottom of the dress. Nicole ran her fingers across the smooth velvet until she reached the silver design. It was softer than she had expected, almost like silk but completely sheer except for hints of silver sparkles. "It's beautiful."

"The design came to me a little late for the Christmas season so I only made a small quantity for New Year's parties, but I believe these two should be the perfect size for Gabriella and Sophia." Wynn took a second one from the pile and laid it beside the first.

"They're perfect. Don't you think, Mac?"

"I think our girls will look adorable in them." Mac rubbed his hand over the small of her back. "Ace was showing off a picture of his daughter, Roulette, with those cute pajamas that say SEALed for You on the shirt. Would you happen to have any in stock?"

"They have the team's name and logo on the back. Those aren't actually something we carry, I've made them especially for the team. Well, the ones who have children, Ace and Gwen and soon Boom and I, but I have the stuff to whip them up. If you could give me until tomorrow I'll have them ready for you."

"That's okay, I'm sure we can find something else. We just need to find something special for our new tradition of new pajamas on Christmas Eve that we'll wear to open gifts in the morning. It's something my parents did with Angelo and me."

"We're starting a number of new Christmas traditions," Nicole explained.

"I did that as a child, it was the one gift we were allowed to open early. My parents were very strict about opening presents early, even the ones from family or friends that were mailed to us." Wynn leaned against the counter. "My favorite part of Christmas was when Ace,

Lucky, and I would band together to search the house for our presents. We never found anything. We later found out that Mom and Dad kept them in Dad's workshop, the one place we weren't allowed without them. It was still fun searching the house."

"Angelo and I did that. One year we found a box in the closet, and thought we stumbled onto the goldmine. That night while our parents were sleeping we snuck down the hall to the living room to open the box, or I should say boxes, because that's all it was. Box after box after box inside of each other. Each wrapped. Inside the last box there was a note: *you thought you could out smart us, did you? You failed, now go back to bed.*" He let out a deep laugh that made him look ten years younger. So full of life and without concern. She had noticed that over their time together he had relaxed more, seeming to have finally let down his guard. This was just another sign of that.

They shared a good laugh before Wynn picked up another garment from the pile. "This is one last dress I thought you might be interested in." The red and white striped shirt with a blue skirt had a white anchor on the right side with the words United States Navy underneath.

"That's adorable, I just love your designs."

"The military designs are specific for this shop, but there's a lot of stuff that I do just for Roulette. I have a bunch of newborn things I've made for my little girl. I can't wait until June when she's born. She'll be my own walking billboard," Wynn joked, once again touching her stomach. "I'd gladly add Gabriella and Sophia to my private list. I have a couple new outfits in the works in support of their daddies."

"Oh, I'd appreciate that." She continued to look through the clothes, setting aside most of the outfits. She knew the girls would quickly outgrow some of them, but they were too adorable to pass up. Shawn did most of the shopping for the girls, so this was her first time experiencing the excitement of shopping for baby clothes, and she was enjoying it. Especially when Mac added his comments, telling her what he liked and didn't.

"Okay. I'll take all of these, plus those pajamas if you're sure you have time to do them." Nicole neatly stacked the clothes she was purchasing.

"I'll have Boom bring them over to the house tomorrow on his way to the airport to pick up my parents."

Mac smirked. "How did Boom get wrapped into that? Shouldn't Ace or Lucky or even you be doing that?"

"Lucky's on duty and Ace made some excuse about taking Gwen and Roulette shopping and then to see Santa." With a smirk, Wynn punched the prices of the garments into the computer. "As for me, well, I have to work."

"Work? I heard you handed the day to day stuff to a manager so you could focus on your designs. With your women's clothing line from Roll of the Diamond already in a number of New York boutiques, and after the first of the year your baby clothes taking over half of a store on Fifth Avenue, I don't think you need to be here. Are you sure it's not an excuse?"

"My sales associate for Heart of Diamond is actually out of town, she won't be returning until after Christmas, and the manager for Roll of the Diamond can't run both stores at the same time. So I have to come in." Wynn put the purchases in a brown bag with the store's logo, diamond design, on the side. "I'll admit I could have closed the shop but Boom owes me one."

"Good for you." Nicole encouraged. "Mac got a dose of my family already."

"It was like water in the face, worse than the cold ocean water during *Hell week*. A doorbell ringing at two in the morning, while the babies are sleeping, is worse than anything the Navy could throw at me," Mac joked.

"My brother, Sam, showed up last night rather unexpectedly," Nicole explained as Mac handed Wynn his credit card. "He's going to stay until after Christmas. Which reminds me, I need to get him a present while we're out."

Mac took hold of the two bags Wynn held out and nodded. "We can head over to the mall next, it might be the best place to find something for him. Plus my gift for Angelo should be in and I can pick it up."

She slipped her hand into Mac's, interlocking their fingers before glancing at Wynn. "Thank you for everything. I can't wait to see what else you design."

"You're welcome. I'll see you at the Christmas party I'm sure," Wynn called to them as they made their way out of the boutique.

"Christmas party…I almost forgot. I'll need to find something to wear."

"Don't worry. I'm sure you'll find something at the mall."

They headed back to the boardwalk, giving her another chance to see the ocean before they reached the car. This time, instead of thinking how beautiful it was, all her thoughts centered on how quickly time was flying by. Before long the holidays would be over and Mac would be back on duty, the threat of deployment hanging over them. She wasn't worried about him being gone, only that she'd miss the time she had with him. The fear of something happening to him lingered.

Her brother's comment from their conversation the night before played in her mind again. *Don't worry about things you can't change. Live each day to the fullest and love with all your heart.*

Mac stood in front of the makeshift work table and sketched out an option for the library. He wanted to give Nicole a few choices to decide from, to make this a place where she could find refuge. The plan was to make the fireplace the center point, with the built-in bookshelves throughout the room sanded down and refinished. He'd take out the built-in end table on each side to expand the window seat to the full length of the window. He'd also add extra depth to the seat so she could cuddle there with the girls.

He was just finishing his notations when the sound of heavy-soled shoes came down the hall and Sam cleared his throat.

"Come in, Sam, and tell me how the call to your parents went. Should I go out there and soothe Nicole?"

"She wanted to get some air, so she stepped outside, and the girls are playing in their playpen."

Mac set the pencil aside and eyed Sam. Since he arrived, he'd changed. No longer did he have the stubble across the face or the chip on his shoulder. There was an understanding between them that was almost becoming a friendship. Considering how close he and Nicole were, it was good that he and Mac could bond. "Then what can I do for you, because I know you didn't come in here just to pass the time of day. Still worried about your sister?"

"I'll always worry about Nicole." Sam ran his hand along the bookshelf, his fingers sliding over the old books that had been left in the house. "She must love this room. Nicole's always been a reader." As if realizing he was straying from the point, he stepped away from the bookcase and turned to face Mac. "Nicole is risking a lot by coming here, not just by putting her life on hold or our parents, but also her happiness. She's leaving behind everyone she knows to come here to be with you and the girls. There's no support system here for her, no one to call in case things go south between the two of you. Yet she's willing to risk it all, not just because of the girls, but because she cares for you. So, before I leave…I want you to know if you hurt my sister, I don't care how much training you have or who has your back, I'll take you down. I won't fail her again."

"I understand where you're coming from. I was raised in an Italian family. We're protective, too. But you have nothing to worry about. I care for Nicole, and for the girls." Mac shoved his hands into his pocket. "Hell, she's already made fast friends with two of my men's wives. Gwen called last night to see if we could plan a play date with her daughter, Roulette, for after Christmas. Then there's Wynn, the owner of the boutique Nicole bought all those clothes from. Nicole won't be alone here, not even when I'm deployed. The military is a tight knit family and the SEAL team even more so. She'll have more support than she's ever had. My parents live close by, so does my brother, they'll be here for her and will help her with the girls when I can't."

"If you break her heart…"

Mac stifled a laugh. Sam cared for Nicole and that was what mattered. He was willing to take Mac on even if he didn't stand a chance. "Threats will do no good. Nicole and I need to explore where things go, but no matter how things turn out in the end we will remain friends for the sake of Gabriella and Sophia. If she wishes to leave and return to Texas, she can do that. I already told her I would keep Shawn's house at least until we we're sure. It would provide her a place to raise the girls if she chooses to return to Texas, and if not it'll be a place we can stay when we visit your family. She has the key and I'd provide a plane ticket any time if that's what she wants."

"What are you two doing in here?" Nicole asked from the doorway.

"Nothing, dear sister." Sam shot Mac a warning glance.

"I've drawn up some ideas for the room. Want to take a look?" Mac grabbed the sketches from the desk and held them out to her. "If you don't like anything, it can be changed. I want this room to be whatever you want."

"I'm excited for it to be done. I'm not exceptionally handy but I'll help in any way I can." She took the papers from him and he slipped his arm around her waist, cuddling her against him. He never pictured himself being happy with a life outside the military, but if anyone could see that he was, it was Nicole.

"I've done some remolding in the past, and I'm here for a few more days. If you want I can give you a hand."

"Sure." Mac and Sam exchanged a glance, as if the two had come to an understanding. It was also another thing they'd have in common besides the fact they both cared for Nicole.

"I guess I'm finishing the Christmas decorating myself. I've been abandoned by both of you in my time of need," she teased.

"It's days before Christmas, why would you want to decorate more when you'll only have to take it down?" Sam raised an eyebrow at her, implying it was a crazy thing to do.

"Mac and I purchased some additional things while we were out. Stuff I wanted to make the house feel homier and make it a special Christmas for all of us. There's garland and lights for around the living room fireplace and main staircase banister. Some other smaller stuff for around the house, including one of those small Christmas trees you plug in and it lights up for the nursery. Remember, we had one in our room."

"She'll have your house looking like Santa's workshop if you let her." Sam shook his head at Nicole's excitement. "I'm surprised she didn't want lights for outside."

"She did but I overruled her."

"You didn't overrule me." She gave Mac a playful jab with her elbow to his stomach. "I saw reason. The outside isn't finished and it's too late to put them up now just to take them down in a few days. Next year we're decorating outside. I don't care if no one will see it from the road, we will."

"Anything you want, *amore*." Mac kissed the top of her head. *Merda*, she had him wrapped around her finger. Oh, how the mighty SEAL had fallen.

Chapter Sixteen

The hour was late when Nicole stepped out the car in front of Mac's dark house. The Christmas party had been wonderful, full of unexpected surprises, and new people. Mac had told her they were a tightknit group, but she didn't truly understand it until tonight. They had accepted her into their fold completely, a tight bond already in place between her and the women. Gwen and Wynn had known each other for years, but it didn't seem to matter to them that Nicole was a newcomer.

She stood there a moment, letting the cold December breeze flow over her, taking her stress with it. She hadn't realized she had been nervous about meeting his fellow SEALs and their families, but now that it was over she was relieved. After talking to the wives, she had a better idea what to expect from the military life. Through uphill battles, deployments, and trainings, she was prepared to stand by him.

Mac wrapped his arm around her waist as they made their way toward the front door and she pressed herself tight against him. "It was a wonderful party."

"I'm glad you had a good time. It was your first introduction into military life, think you can handle it?"

She waited until they were at the top of the steps before turning to him so they were face to face, and leaned close. "I can do anything to be with you."

"You don't know how happy that makes me." He leaned down, pressing his lips to hers.

"Take me upstairs, I want you to make love to me again."

He slipped the key into the lock and opened the door. "I thought you'd never ask." He bent down and scooped her into his arms.

"I can walk."

"I have no doubt, *amore*." He kicked the door shut behind him and flicked the deadbolt, all with her in his arms. "You're mine. *Sempre*."

As he carried her up the stairs, she ran her hands over his chest, and she couldn't help but like the sound of the words he spoke. "It's so sexy when you speak in Italian." He whispered something in Italian against her ear but she couldn't make out the meaning of it. Instead, it seemed to have a direct line to her core. He could have said anything and it wouldn't matter. It wasn't about the words, but the way he said it.

In the master bedroom, he laid her on the bed and went to shut the door. "I want you naked."

"So demanding," she teased, echoing the very words he'd said to her.

"When I want something, nothing will stand in my way, including a few shreds of cloth." He pulled off his shirt and began working his belt through the loops of his dress slacks. "Now come on, there's something I want to show you." He stripped off the rest of his clothes, only leaving his boxers in place before going to the closet.

"Where are we going?"

"The stairway to the stars. Now come on." He disappeared inside the walk-in closet.

"You don't seriously thing I'm going to have sex in a closet, do you?" She slipped her little black dress off, pulled off the stockings she hated, and still there was no sign of him. "Mac, I'm serious."

"You're going to miss out if you don't come in here." Following Mac's words was a creak of wood. "Come on, *amore*. I won't wait all night before I throw you over my shoulder and carry you in here."

She slipped off the bed and padded toward the closet. "Mac, don't you think the bed would be more comfortable?" She glanced around but all she could see was clothes and space. Where did he disappear to?

Mac stuck his head out of what she thought was a wall, but had to be a hidden doorway. "I do. Now come along, I promise you won't regret it."

"Where the hell are you going? Where does that door go?"

"I already told you, it's the stairway to the stars, now are you coming?" He held his hand out to her. "Tonight I'm going to make love to you under the stars."

"It's too cold to be outside."

"Just trust me and come on."

She placed her hand in his and let him pull her toward the door. "Stairs." The word emerged soft and full of surprise.

"My CO has faith I can lead my men, but you doubt me when I tell you we're on the stairway to the stars. What little confidence you have in me, *amore*." He nodded for her go to first. "Watch your head at the top."

"I have every confidence in you but this is impossible. I've seen it from the outside. There's not enough room for another floor." She took the stairs slowly, her mind running with the possibilities of what she'd find.

"It's not another floor in strict terms. It's an attic of sorts that is only accessible from this room, but trust me it's something you won't regret. Now get those legs moving or I'm going to take you on the stairs. Those sexy bikini bottoms are calling my name, and you waving that sexy ass in my face is only making me hotter."

"I'm not having the steps dig into my back." She sped her pace, watching the slant of the roof as she neared the top. The chill in the air hit her and she felt her nipples hardening. "It's a little cold."

"No worries, I'm going to warm you up."

There in the middle of the space was a full size mattress completely made, but what caught her eye was above it. A huge skylight, letting in the moonlight and all the stars. "It's beautiful."

"It's not much, only a mattress on the floor, but when I can't sleep or just need an escape I come up here. When you're lying under the stars, you realize how small you really are in this world. After tonight, there seemed to be no better place than this to make love to you."

She reached back, unhooked her bra, and lay down on the center of the bed. "Well, what are you waiting for?"

With a playful grin etched onto the contours of his face, Mac wasted no time stripping his boxers. Naked, he crawled onto the bed next to her. She reached out to touch him, to draw her hands over his perfect body.

"*Bella, amore.*" Mac leaned over her, kissing a path down to her breasts before he feverishly claimed her hard nipple. He slid his other hand down her body, caressing her thigh before he spread her legs.

She dug her nails into his back until he looked up at her. "Please…" He pushed her legs farther apart until he had enough room to slip between them, his stiff shaft pressed against her inner thigh.

"All in due time, *amore.*" Before she could respond, he pressed his lips to hers, his tongue diving deep between her lips. He slipped his fingers between her legs and thrust into her tightness, making her squirm with delight as he used his thumb to massage her clit. She moaned around his unrelenting kiss, clawing at his shoulders with her nails, until finally his teeth grazed her lower lip and he pulled back enough to let her cries of frustration escape.

"I need you now."

He hovered above her, angling between her spread thighs, his shaft teasing along her entrance without entering as he watched her.

"You're beautiful…with the moonlight reflecting off your skin, even more so." As if that single statement snapped the last of his control, he drove into her with one powerful thrust. He gave her no time to catch her breath before he began rocking in and out.

She arched into him, her body pressed against his and placed kisses along the arch of his neck. Her teeth grazed over the pulse of his neck that beat frantically. Pleasure built within her until the ecstasy began to overwhelm her. She wrapped her arms around his neck, holding onto him with every pump, until her body exploded around him. He continued to drive his shaft into her, slamming home with more urgency than before. Her inner muscles clenched around him, tightening until each pump felt like too much. Until with one final thrust, he called her name.

With him still buried deep within her, she collapsed back against the mattress, her breaths coming in hard, fast pants. "That was amazing."

He slipped out of her, leaving her with an emptiness, and lay down next to her. His leg over hers, he pulled her tight against his body. "You're amazing."

They laid there snuggled together watching the sky. Never before did the star constellations seem so clear. "This would be beautiful when there's a meteor shower."

"It is, but nothing compared to the beauty beside me." He kissed her temple. "Who knew something as horrible as death could bring me three wonderful blessings? You're more than I could have ever hoped for, and the twins are pure angels. Nicole, I love you."

He loves me. She ran her hand down his cheek, their gazes locked together. "Oh, Mac, all my life I wanted something like this and now I have it. I love you."

"I told you I thought this Christmas would be the best one for all of us. We're a family." He trailed his fingers along her hip and up her body.

"There's just one thing…"

"Anything, *amore*. Just name it."

She bit her lip, unsure how to put her one worry into words without making her sound ungrateful. "Not right now, but I want kids of our own. Don't take that wrong, I mean the girls are ours and I don't love them any less because I didn't give birth to them, but I want to experience the joy of birth myself."

"I understand, and we can have as many as you want. A whole house full and if we ever outgrow this place we'll find a bigger house or add on." He tugged a blanket from the edge of the bed and pulled it over them. "I don't want to spoil the evening, but you've been distant. What's on your mind?"

"I was thinking about Sam. He took a lot of Mom's anger on the phone yesterday to shield me, but he's going to have to deal with it when he gets back home. He'll only be there one day before he has to report back to the rig. I wish my parents would just accept this."

"This situation, you mean?" When she looked up at him, he continued. "I overheard you remind Sam before the call to your parents that you didn't want to tell them about us. Why?"

Guilt poured through her. "I'm sorry."

"There's no need to apologize, I just want to know why."

"Since my first date when Dad exploded because the boy tried to kiss me, I keep my personal life away from my parents." Her hand left his chest and moved to the scar. "If I date someone, that's my business and no one else's. Sam is another matter altogether, he won't have it. He feels the need to approve any man in my life."

"Angelo and I would do the same if we had a sister. Just wait until Gabriella and Sophia are dating." He let out a joyous laugh at the thought.

"What a nightmare that will be. Between you, Angelo, and Sam, any boys they bring around will be scared out of their minds. I'd be surprised if the girls even get a kiss before they're twenty, because of all the fear you'd have put into them."

"Who said they'd be allowed to date before they were twenty-one? Or maybe I'll send them to a convent and my girls can be nuns."

"Not on your life." She tipped her head and kissed his lips. "Our daughters will have a good head on their shoulders and will make the right decisions. One day they'll find men just like their daddy, because I couldn't hope for a better man for them."

The words *just like their daddy* tore at Mac's heart. He wanted better men for Gabriella and Sophia, men who were stronger and didn't let people down. His actions and choice had gotten men killed. The girls deserved someone better than him.

Hell, Nicole deserved someone better than him but he couldn't tear himself away from her. He wanted her like nothing he'd ever wanted before, and he'd go to the ends of the earth to keep her in his arms. Nicole was the woman he dreamed about, until he realized marriage and the military didn't mix. He'd seen too many divorces over the years. But he was sure this relationship was going to work, he could sense it. They had more to fight for, more on the line, and more importantly, they came into this knowing it wouldn't always be easy, but it would always be worth fighting for. Their little family meant everything to him.

A star shot across the sky, leaving a trail of light in its wake. As if it transported him back to his childhood when he believed in simple things, he made a wish that everything would work out for his little family. That he could keep Nicole in his arms and Gabriella and Sophia safe. That he'd do right by Shawn in raising the girls, and he and Sam would never have to come to blows over Nicole's happiness. A happy family and future.

Chapter Seventeen

Christmas Eve was upon them. As Nicole and her new family sat in the living room with the Christmas tree lighting up the room, she cherished where the year had brought them. In Mac's safe embrace slept Gabriella, unaware what a special night this was, while Sophia rested against her Uncle Sam's chest as he read her a Christmas tale.

She couldn't believe what changes the year had brought her. In January, she had her accounting firm; business was great but she was miserable. It wasn't what she wanted any longer. The numbers that had always been her thing had lost their appeal. She wanted a life outside the endless hours, something that would provide daily challenges. Little did she know that by summer she'd have closed the firm's doors and a week later would be a nanny. It hadn't been what she went to school for, but she was happy. Though that happiness was nothing compared to what she had now.

New Year's Day would bring another year but it would also be seven months since the girls were born and her freedom from routine. In seven months Gabriella and Sophia had blossomed into beautiful little girls and she had been a part of that.

Thank you, Shawn, for placing that ad in the paper and for giving me a chance even though I had no experience.

She curled her legs under her and snuggled closer to Mac. "These sleepy little girls should be put to bed."

"I think Gabriella is sleeping fine and Sophia seems to be enjoying the story. Why not wait a bit? It's a quiet evening, surrounded by those we love." Mac kept his voice low so as not to disturb the girls.

"All right, just a little longer." She rested her head against his shoulder. The doorbell echoed through the space, startling her. "Expecting someone?"

"No. Here, take Gabriella and I'll answer it."

"No way, she's asleep. I'll get the door." She unfolded her legs and stood. "You keep still and let her sleep." She pushed off the sofa and strolled toward the door.

"Check the peephole before you open it," Mac called to her.

"This isn't the first time I opened a door at night." Sam had made sure she had enough street smarts to keep her safe. She checked the door and could just barely make out Angelo through mountains of presents. "It's Angelo."

"What is he doing here?" Mac questioned.

She pulled open the door, and Angelo stepped inside, handing an armload of presents to her before he reached back outside the doorway and grabbed his Santa sack. He had a red velvet Santa outfit on with a pillow stuffed up under the jacket to give him a big belly, a black belt around his waist and a white beard completing the outfit. "Santa's here."

"What are you doing?" Mac twisted around to see his brother and tried not to laugh at the sight.

"You said you wanted to make this Christmas special for the girls. Well, Santa has made a special call to see the García twins."

"Aww, Santa." Nicole held back the tears that threatened to fall.

"I won't have any of that. Now come along and be my little elf so I can see these special girls." Angelo didn't wait for her, instead he headed straight for Sophia who was watching him with such joy that her little feet were kicking in excitement. He sat his bag aside and reached down to lift Sophia from Sam's arms. "Little Sophia, have you been a good girl?" He held the girl out in his arms, checking her over. "I'd say you've been keeping your Mommy and Daddy busy, haven't you?"

"I'm going to grab my camera." Sam dashed off to his bedroom in order to get the camera he never left home without. Photography was one of his hobbies and he had such an eye for it that he'd sold a number of his pictures.

"You almost didn't make it in time, Nicole wanted to put them to bed." Mac held out a hand to her, to bring her back next to him.

"I believe I missed Gabriella. You must have worn her out today." Angelo sat and bounced Sophia on his knee.

"She was up earlier than Sophia this morning," Mac explained, glancing down at Gabriella who was missing all the fun. "We'll have to wake her up so she doesn't miss Santa's visit."

"Just give me a couple minutes to get a few pictures of Sophia with Santa first." Sam came into the room, his camera at the ready.

"Sam, maybe you should think about moving here. Without you, I'm not sure if I'd have any good pictures of the girls." She glanced at Mac. "You should see the ones he took of them so far. Every three weeks while he was off the rig, he'd come over and take pictures of the girls. The scrapbook I brought with me has some beautiful photos of them."

"Have you considered making that your living?" Mac asked.

"Not me." Sam shook his head. "It's a passion but that's all it is. I don't want to be stuck with the pressure of finding that perfect picture for weddings, events, or family pictures. I do the pictures of the girls because they are growing so fast. When they first came home from the hospital they were so tiny and now look at them. The pictures will be a timeline of their life, something to look back on. Nowadays so many people don't take pictures to remember their lives. It's a shame." He snapped away, moving as needed to get a better picture as Santa Angelo and Sophia shared their moment.

She reached over and ran her hands over Gabriella's stomach. "Come on, sweetie, you need to wake up, Santa's here to see you." As Gabriella's eyes opened, Nicole lifted her into her arms. "That's it, sweetie. Look Santa."

As if she understood who the man in the red suit was, Gabriella reached out to him with one arm while she rubbed her eyes with the other. Baby chatter was shared between the twins as Nicole placed Gabriella in Angelo's other arm.

"Perfect, right there." Sam knelt, snapping more pictures with both girls on Santa's lap.

When the girls found Angelo's fake beard, their laughter and smiles made Sam's clicks of the camera faster. Not a moment of this was going to be missed thanks to her brother and his ever ready camera. Memories to cherish for years to come.

Mac came to stand by her, his arm around her waist, as they watched the scene unfold. "I think we've found Angelo's job for years to come, because the girls must have Santa visit them on Christmas Eve. It's now part of our traditions."

"Hear that Angelo, you've become the official Santa for the García family." Mac laughed when Angelo looked up at him, a hint of fear in his eyes. "Wait until there's a house full of children."

"I can see the headlines, Santa mauled at the García house, next at five." Angelo tipped his head back and let out a deep laugh. "*Cazzo*, I'm screwed."

"Watch your mouth." Mac eyed his brother. "We're going to teach the girls Italian and I don't want that to be their first word."

"What's *Cazzo*?" When neither of them answered her, Nicole turned to face Mac. "Well…"

"Fuck."

It took her a moment to realize that was the translation, not him bitching about having to translate it. "Oh yeah, none of that around my innocent girls."

"Their father is a SEAL and I'm a Marine, do you honestly think they will not hear this stuff?" Angelo watched her before adding, "Just know these little girls have a bunch of big and powerful men watching over them."

"I might not be military but no harm will come to my nieces under my watch." Sam sat his camera aside.

"I never doubted it for a moment Sam." She smiled at her brother, knowing the girls had two amazing uncles to protect them if anything ever happened to her, or Mac. "Now I should get these girls to bed so Santa can put out the presents for morning."

"One more picture, I want to get one with the four of you. The first picture of the new family."

"Oh, Sam, shouldn't we do that tomorrow when we're all dressed for Christmas dinner at Mac's parents' house?" She hated taking pictures and at least wanted to be wearing something nicer than jeans and a long sleeve shirt.

"We will tomorrow but you need a family picture with Santa." He tipped his head. "Now come on."

"Come on, *amore*. Our first family picture and tomorrow we'll have another one, more formal, to put on the wall." Mac led them forward.

The first official sign that they were a family made her heart flutter. "All right, but Santa's chair needs to move, I want it in front of the tree. We need to have the Christmas tree with the light glimmering behind us. Then I want you to put that on time delay and get in the picture with us."

She wanted the picture to remind her of this night because in two days Sam would be on his way back to Texas. They'd still be close but distance would separate them. Visits would be few and far between when he left. So many milestones would be missed. The sadness of the loss coursed within her, casting a shadow over their Christmas celebration.

With the girls asleep for the night in the nursery, Nicole had a moment alone with Sam while Mac and Angelo were discussing the entertainment space in the basement. They sat in the living room, the tree casting the only light while Sam drank a beer.

"Out with it, sis. I know something's on your mind." Sam took a swig from his beer bottle.

"You've always known me so well." She turned to face him, bringing her legs up onto the sofa to hug them to her body. "I've been thinking about you going back to Texas."

"If you're worried about Mom, don't be. I can handle her. She's upset because she feels you're wasting your life by caring for children that aren't yours when you worked so hard to put yourself through college. But I know this is more than just your love for the girls. You love Mac." When she opened her mouth to say something, he stopped her. "Don't deny it. I've seen the way you two look at each other."

"I wasn't going to deny it. You're right...I do love him." She ran her hands down her legs. "That's not what's on my mind. I know you can handle Mom, and honestly after the holidays I'm going to tell Mom about Mac and me. Maybe that will get her to ease up. No, I've been thinking about you. You took the job on the oil rig to get out of the house and help Mom with the medical bills from Dad's treatment and then his heart attack."

"What's your point?"

"I know you're not happy doing that work and there's so much you miss being on that rig for three weeks at a time. Why don't you move here? There's plenty of space here until you get on your feet, and Mac could use the help with the house."

"Mac doesn't want me around, he'd rather keep you all to himself." Sam brought the bottle to his lips but didn't take a sip. "If this came up because you think I won't visit, I promise I will."

"Actually, it was Mac's idea. With his squad having time off for the holidays it means his rotation will be up next for any mission that comes along. The chances of him being deployed after the first of the year are high. Having you close…well, it would mean a lot to me and it would give Mac more piece of mind."

"Angelo and his parents are close, plus the women you spoke of, Wynn and Gwen. You won't be alone."

"This isn't about me being alone. You're right, I do have his family and the military wives. This is about me wanting you close and wanting you happy. If you were happy on that rig I wouldn't even approach the subject, but come on, Sam…you're not." She tucked her legs under her and leaned forward. "Angelo and his parents are great and I know if I needed something they'd be there. Angelo is a JAG officer for the Marines, his hours are long, but there's always Maria and Tony. They'll be a part of the twins' lives, but it won't replace their Uncle Sam."

"This is your life. You're just starting out."

"I don't know what that has to do with anything. You're my brother and I love you. Mom and Dad are settled there, they have their lives, but we don't have to stay there. Mac's keeping Shawn's house, we can use it whenever we want to see them. It's time for you to start living your life and stop thinking about everyone else. If you don't want to start over here, go anywhere you want, but it's time for you to stop working a job you hate."

He set his beer aside and glared at her. "You're more outspoken than you used to be."

"All I'm asking is for you to think about it." She straightened her back and returned his glare. "There's more to life than making a living. Look what happened when I gave up my career, it brought me a family of my own and a man I love."

"Not everyone is so lucky." He picked up his beer again and took another long drink.

"You won't know unless you try and you'll never find love if you're locked up on that rig three weeks at a time. It's time for you to live your own life. It doesn't hurt that if you're here the girls will have their Uncle Sam in their lives regularly. You mean a lot to me and the girls need you. Please just think about it."

"Okay, I'll think about it."

Even with his agreement, she didn't have hopes that anything would come of it. Sam was too stubborn for him to give up his career without something to fall back on, and he wouldn't let his sister convince him to give up providing for their parents when things became tough. He'd work his life away on that rig if it kept everyone happy, even if he was miserable. Though she wasn't about to give up. She'd see that he found the same happiness that she found with Mac. Even if it took her last breath.

Chapter Eighteen

Christmas morning had come at last and with the first rays of sunlight Nicole's eyes popped open. It might be their last Christmas morning that they could sleep in, because with two little girls the idea of Christmas and presents would get them up earlier. Next year they'd be a year and a half old; the holiday season would be more fun as they'd tear open their own gifts.

"Morning, *amore*." Mac whispered, snuggling closer, his head pressed against hers while his teeth claimed her earlobe.

"We have no time for that this morning."

"We can make time. Sam and Angelo can handle the girls if they wake up." Mac slid his hand under the blanket to slide along the curve of her body. "It works out nicely that Angelo was tired and wanted to see the girls open their gifts. Now he's here and can help Sam look after the girls while I give you a proper Christmas present."

"How about sex in the shower? Than we won't be interrupted and when I first saw that shower all I could think about was making love pressed against glass while the rainfall showerhead covers us with warm water." She slipped from the bed and held out her hand to him.

"Come on. I've always wanted to make love under a waterfall, this is as close as I'll get."

"It takes a minute for the water to warm up. Why don't you wait in bed under the warm blanket and I'll get it started." He gave her a kiss that promised more to come and strolled away, his shaft already standing to attention.

"I'm cold without you," she hollered toward the bathroom as the water turned on.

"I promise I'll make it worth the wait."

"You better." She pulled the blanket tight around her. Every ounce of her wanted to go to him, she didn't care if the water was cold, she just wanted to make every moment count.

"*Amore.*"

She stripped the blanket off and padded quickly toward the shower. The sight of him already inside the glass enclosure, water running down his naked body, stopped her in her tracks. *Damn he's a fine specimen of manhood, and he's all mine.* Not waiting a moment longer, she stepped in under the jets of hot water until they cascaded down her body. She closed her eyes, putting her head under the powerful showerhead and letting the water rinse away the chill.

Once the chill was gone she opened her eyes and found Mac standing there before her with a sneaky grin on his face.

"I believe you promised this would be worth my wait."

"That I did." He nodded, his gaze watching her with intensity.

She waited but when he made no move to touch her she gave into temptation and ran her hands down his slippery chest. "I thought you wanted to make this the best Christmas of my life. Time to man up, SEAL."

"You couldn't be more right there." He knelt in front of her, the water cascading over him. "All my life I've been dedicated to the Navy, to my men, and to saving others, little did I know that one day you'd come along and save me. What we have between us is something I've seen others have but I never thought I'd find. It's beyond anything I could have imaged and I refuse to let it pass me by. I'm an old sea-battled, weatherworn SEAL and still you've shown me there's more to life than just the military. I love you, Nicole Marie Ryan. Will you do me the honor of marrying me?" He slipped a beautiful princess diamond ring with an infinity-swirled band from the palm of his hand.

"Oh, Mac!" Tears slid down her face, mixing with the hot water. "Yes."

He slid the ring onto her finger and stood up. "I know this is happening fast, but things have never been clearer for me before. You're the woman I want to spend the rest of my life with."

She pressed her index finger to his lips. "If it was happening too fast I'd have said no. I love you and I want to spend the rest of my life with you. Now I think a celebration is in order." With a wiggle of her eyebrows, she pulled him closer.

He took a step, advancing on her and pressing her against the shower wall. "*Amore*, someday you're going to wear this old man out."

"Not a chance." She ran her hands over his wet chest. "You can't deny you want this is much as I do." She glared up at him.

Without delay, he crushed his mouth to hers, and slid his hand between her legs. A moan pealed from between her lips as he found her core. He held her captive against the cool titled wall, drawing her closer to orgasm. She moaned around his unrelenting kiss. Fierce desire rose within her like a tidal wave smashing through a dam.

"I want you." She murmured against his mouth, holding onto him as wild delight eddied through her.

His teeth grazed her lower lip and he pulled his hand away. She cried out in frustration, but he ignored her demands. Gripping her hips, he lifted her and spread her thighs before he drove into her with one powerful thrust. He gave her no time to catch her breath before he began rocking in and out of her. Her body tight with desire and a building climax, she had no control, as he left her mouth and kissed a path along her neck. She dug into his shoulders, holding on to him as every pump of his hips sent pulses of pleasure exploding through her. She came apart at the seams, her inner muscles clenching to him as he continued to drive into her.

He slammed home in a frenzy and his climax burst through as a second tsunami shattered her world. She shook with the force of it. If it wasn't for his support she would have collapsed into a heap on the shower floor.

The water turned cold and he shut it off, sliding free of her slowly and reluctantly. Her mind was almost numb, raw sensation skittering through her. Wrapping her in a towel, he carried her out of the shower, placing her on the bathroom counter, then dried her off.

"If I had the energy I'd have you take me right here on the counter so I could see it in the mirrors." She wrapped her arms around his neck.

"I'll add it to my list. Once the weather is nicer I want to make love to you by the creek that's just beyond the trees."

"Promises, promises." She moaned and dragged her nails along his back. "But now I think we must get dressed. I can hear Sophia giving her uncles a hard time."

"They can handle the girls for a little bit longer while I spend a few more minutes alone with my fiancée. After all, it's Christmas morning, aren't we entitled to make them earn their keep?" He lifted her off the counter and stood her in front of him.

"Isn't making Angelo sleep in the guest room that's not complete, and is more storage than an actual bedroom, payment enough?" She laughed at the thought of what her future brother-in-law had slept in.

"He's a Marine, he's slept in worse." He wrapped his arms around her and tugged her close to his body. "My fiancée, I can't believe it. I love you."

"I love the sound of fiancée but I think I'll love wife more."

"You just let me know when. Hell, if you want to do it tomorrow I'll be there," he teased.

"Not tomorrow but I don't want to wait too long." She let her head fall against his hard chest, enjoying the sensation of his body against hers. All her life she had wanted this and each step she took on the path of life brought her here. It saddened her knowing that death had brought him to his happiness, but she wouldn't have changed the outcome for the world.

To dress the girls in their Christmas outfits was easier said than done. They wanted nothing to do with the cute black velvet dress with the sparkly, silver sheer tie around the waist, no matter how much Nicole and Sam fussed to get them into them. She didn't even want to think about the cute silver barrettes she had purchased to complete the outfit. As she slid the dress over Gabriella's head, the little girl's arms flew like wild trying to keep it off. "You stop this right now, or you'll both be going naked."

"Are they always this hard to dress?" Sam hadn't even gotten the dress over Sophia's head and was looking more flustered than she had ever seen him.

"They love being naked almost as much as they love bath time and splashing in the water." She leaned down until she was at eye level with the girls. "It's Christmas, we've got to go see your Nana and Poppy. Let's put them down on the play mat for a few minutes and they can burn some of the energy, then we'll try it again. A few minutes from now, they'll forget all about being naked."

"Just wait until they realize they can take off their diapers. Then you're in deep trouble." He chuckled. After placing Sophia on the play mat, he shoved his hands into the pockets of his dress slacks. "So, when were you planning to tell me?"

"Tell you what?" She laid Gabriella next to Sophia under the dangling toys.

"You've never been a good liar." He glanced to her hand. "Ring finger, left hand."

"Aww…" She ran her thumb over the ring and twisted it before turning it the right way around. "Mac asked me this morning and I said yes. What more is there to tell?"

"How about telling your brother? Shouting it from the rooftops? That's what people normally do when they're engaged."

"It's Christmas, it's more about family and the holidays than Mac and I. Don't you approve of him? Oh, Sam, please be happy for me, I love him."

"I approve of him. Actually, I'm not sure if I could have picked anyone better. Maybe younger, but not better." Sam paused, looking at the girls before his gaze returned to her. "I haven't said anything about the age difference before now, but you know Mom and Dad will have an issue with it. Dad will probably have a fit when he finds out. How are you going to deal with them?"

"The way I've always dealt with them, on my own terms. This is my life and I'm living it. Mom's already not happy with me living here in Virginia with Mac and raising the twins, this is just another thing she can be upset about. Or she can look at it as the life she wanted me to have. She's been telling me I should find a man of my own, get married, and have a few children. I'm doing it."

"Speaking of children, how old is Mac?"

"Don't start about his age. He'll be forty in January, and I understand there's an age gap, but that doesn't matter if you love someone."

Sam held his hands out in front of him. "I only meant there could come a day when you're stuck raising the girls on your own, same with any kids the two of you would have together. Are you prepared for that?"

"No one is guaranteed tomorrow, but if you're concerned about me raising kids and having to go back to work, don't be. Shawn was very successful when it came to his business endeavors. Before we got engaged, Mac offered that if I wanted to leave with the girls and return to Texas that he'd have it transferred to me. Money won't be a concern." She ran her hand over the back of her dress and sat down on the small sofa in the nursery. "Losing him would be heartbreaking for me, or I should say us. The girls have been through too much, but sometimes you must love no matter the risks."

Sam came to her and took her hands in his. "I told you before I support you and I couldn't have hoped you'd have found a better man, I only wanted you to understand the risks. I'm happy for you, everything you've ever wanted you've gone after, and now you have it."

"Some risks are worth taking. *You* can be happy if you want." She squeezed his hand. "No pressure, I'm just saying."

"I told you I'd give it some thought, and I have been...but I'm not ready to make a decision yet."

She nodded because there was nothing else she could do. She'd already told him what she thought he should do. Now it was time to leave it in his hands and see what he decided. It was his life and he had to live it himself. She had her hands full dealing with her own life and the changes that would still be coming.

"Nicole, Sam, your mother is on the phone and is demanding to speak with one of you *now*," Mac said from the doorway, holding the phone out to them.

"I'll deal with them, after all I have something to tell them. Can you help Sam get the girls ready?"

"I feel like I've just received grunt duty." He leaned down and picked up Sophia. "Come on, *bella*, we must get you ready for Nana's."

With the girls in safe hands, she stepped into the hallway and brought the phone to her ear. "Merry Christmas, Mom."

"It's not a Merry Christmas with my children across the country. You should be here with us."

"Why? We've never celebrated the holidays. You and Dad have always gone to a friend's party on Christmas." Nicole let out a sigh and made her way farther down the hall to their bedroom, out of hearing range. Now that her mother was on the phone, she decided to get her news out in the open instead of waiting until after the holidays. "Mom, I don't want to fight. It's Christmas, I've got good news I want to share, and I promise we'll come for a visit after the New Year."

"What is your news?" Her mother asked with little interest. She heard something clink in the background.

Nicole could picture her mother at her dressing table getting ready for the big Christmas party. She took a deep breath and decided the best way to tell her mother was to just get it out. "Mac and I are getting married."

"Married!" Something cluttered before her mother gathered herself. "He didn't even have the nerve to meet your parents or ask for your father's hand in marriage before he asked you? What kind of man are you marrying?"

"Mom, we've never been that kind of family. He's a good man, and Sam likes him, but more to the point I love him."

"You love him? You just met him. I'm assuming this is the same man who showed up to claim the girls. The SEAL who's old enough to be your father."

She took a deep breath and pushed her anger aside. "He's not. Mac is thirty-nine, and yes, that's the man I'm marrying. You can decide to be supportive, or fight this at every crossroad. Whatever your choice, know it will affect you being a part of my life and grandparents to your granddaughters. I love you and Dad but it's time I think of my family. If you're going to be negative about Mac, it will affect my girls, and I won't have it."

"Sam would never speak to me that way."

"You might be right, Mom, but you've raised me to be independent and think for myself. You wanted me to fight for what I believe in. That's what I'm doing now. If you give Mac a chance, I know you'd like him." She leaned against the closed bedroom door. "You wanted me to get married, to have a family of my own. I'm doing that."

"I didn't mean marry the first man you saw."

"I'm not. I'm marrying the man I fell in love with. Mom, please be happy for me."

Her mother was silent for a long time before finally asking, "When's the wedding?"

"We haven't set a date. He just asked me this morning, but sometime after the New Year. We know this is what we want so we're not going to wait long. I hope you'll come here for the wedding." She wasn't sure when she decided it, but the wedding would be in Virginia, not Texas. It made more sense and she was fond of the idea of a beach wedding or at least something with a view, maybe at sunset.

She half listened to her mother ramble on about weddings, children, and marriage in general, but her mind was on other things. The least of them was her mother's halfhearted approval, only to keep another fight at bay. While her mother talked, she considered ideas for the wedding and the house. The garage...

Chapter Nineteen

Suddenly everything was clear. It was the one piece she was missing to convince Sam to move to Virginia, and now she had it. "Mom, I've got to go. Sophia is getting into stuff and she's dressed for Christmas dinner. Tell Dad I love him, and Merry Christmas. I'll call you again soon." She didn't wait for her mother's response before hanging up and jogging back down the hall to the nursery.

"Mom have you running for the hills?" Sam stood with Gabriella in his arms, looking as adorable as ever in her Christmas dress.

She shook her head. "The garage."

"What?" Sam looked at her as if she'd gone mad, even Mac had turned to her in question as he finished placing a barrette in Sophia's hair.

"You've always wanted to buy Johnson's garage. That was your dream until you went to work on that rig. Why not do it. Now's your chance."

"There's a lot of start-up money involved in a garage, and without customers it will fail. It's too big of a risk." He shook his head. "Plus, Johnson sold his garage years ago, there's a young guy running the place now and from what I hear it's not doing too well. He's ripping people off."

"That's just it, Sam. People need good mechanics that won't rip them off."

"You're missing the point. Most of what I earned for the first few years went to paying Dad's bills. I have money saved, but not enough for that."

"I understand what you're getting at." Mac nodded. "Tell him about the garage and I'll take the girls downstairs."

"Stay, you're as much a part of this as I am. Family, remember." She turned to Sam and tipped her head to the window. "The garage, it's completely set up, even has a lift, everything you need."

"Oh no, Nicole." Sam shook his head and looked to Mac for support. "This is your home, you don't want people tramping through here day in and day out. Think of the girls and the noise."

"Noise wouldn't be an issue, I insulated and soundproofed it. Being a SEAL, I never know when I'll be called up, so I sleep when I can between missions and trainings. One thing I never wanted was some damn bird chirping and waking me up."

"Mac showed me the garage when he gave me the grand tour, and mentioned that he thought about renting it out. It's just sitting there waiting for someone—you—to use it."

"I don't know." Sam looked down at the little girl in his arms. "You'd like to have your Uncle Sam close, wouldn't you?"

"She can't answer, so can I answer for them?" Nicole stepped closer to Sam. "I know I'm pushing and I said I wouldn't, but I want to see you happy. I feel it starts with you putting your notice in on the rig, and beginning a new life. You'd make a wonderful mechanic."

"There's an apartment above the garage, two bedrooms, two baths. Pretty nice, but needs a little work," Mac added. "When I'm away, you'd be close to watch over Nicole and the girls, to keep them safe."

"Okay." Sam's voice was edged with resolve. "I'll put my notice in when I return. They request I do thirty days but I have some vacation time left, so I should be able to do less time on the rig. I'll need to go pack up and tell our parents. Then I'll drive here, so if there's anything else you need from Texas let me know and I can bring it, but I should be back by the end of January. I hope you won't regret this, Nicole."

"Never." She drew Sam into a hug. "I love you, big brother."

"As I love you, little sister." He lifted Gabriella higher into his arms. "You hear that, little one? Your Uncle Sam is going to be living just across the driveway. So any little boys who come around had better watch it."

"Yeah, when Daddy's away, Uncle Sam will scare them off because they're not allowed to date *ever*." Mac came to stand next to Nicole and put his arm around her waist. "Actually, Wynn dropped off these little onesies that says just that. On the back it says, *don't test my daddy, he's a Navy SEAL*. They are wrapped and in the car so they can be opened at Mom's. Can't wait to see her face."

"You're evil. Do you know that, Mac García?"

"You know there's still a big chance the garage will fail," Sam pointed out. "I don't know anyone here to—"

"Don't think like that. It's going to work out, I have faith in you." She laid her hand on Sam's arm. "If you'd like I could create a website for you, do your accounting, place your orders, whatever you need."

"My office girl, hmm…who'd have thought," Sam teased.

"We have a board on base with different business cards. If you get some made up I'll put them there." Sophia's giggled and reached for Nicole, but Mac only shook his head at her and kept the little girl tucked against his body. "I know someone who works at the Family Readiness System, it's basically the one place you go for any support and services, and it's there to promote readiness for deployments. One of their biggest jobs is relocation. When a service member gets a new permanent duty station, they're the ones to answer all the questions. Sometimes new people move into the area and they are looking for services, like mechanics. I'll leave some of your cards there."

"Thank you." Sam nodded.

"See, before long you'll be bursting with work. Now, come on, we better get these girls to Nana's before they need a nap." She reached out to Gabriella. "Want me to take her?"

"She's fine." Sam kissed the top of Gabriella's head. "I need all the uncle time I can get before I leave tomorrow."

"You won't be gone long," she reminded him.

Mac stepped toward the door as if reminding them they needed to be going. "I can either move one of the car seats to the third row so you won't be stuck between them, or Sam can take my truck and follow us. It's pretty much a straight shot, so if you take my truck you could come back here early if you wish. Angelo already left. He wanted to change before going to Mom's, so he'll meet us there."

"I know moving the car seats are troublesome. I'll take your truck if you don't mind, no use causing the girls more heartache by separating them in the car when they don't care for it much anyway." He glanced down at Gabriella. "I never did understand why you and your sister didn't like car rides. That puts most babies to sleep, but not you two. My difficult nieces."

"I just hope they grow out of it." She placed her hand on the doorframe and turned back to Sam. "I think we can spare five minutes so you can look at the garage before we go."

"I already told you I'd move, what more do you want?" Sam teased.

"She's very demanding isn't she?" Mac called over his shoulder as he made his way down the steps.

"Just because you've got the training to back you, doesn't mean I won't hurt you, Mac." She shook her head at her fiancée. "Did you remember the diaper bag?"

"It's in here," Mac called from the living room as she came down the steps. "Will you come grab it?"

She strolled through the space, her heels clicking off the floor, but what she noticed most was the way Mac stood there rocking Sophia, his eyes twinkling with anticipation. "What's going on?" He didn't answer, only nodded to the diaper bag, where a white box with a red ribbon sat on top of it.

"I had planned to give it to you this morning but with all the excitement I waited for a quiet moment. I considered doing it at my parents' house, but with Sam getting the garage and moving here I feel it's best that you open it now."

"You've already given me so much." She looked down at the box.

"Then consider it from Shawn and the twins. I'm only playing a small part in it." He nodded to the box. "Open it."

Timidly she picked up the smooth box and let her fingers run across the lid before she pulled the thick red ribbon that held it closed. Inside she found two keys. "What's this for?"

"The cottage."

Her legs nearly gave out from under her before she was able to take a step to the right and sit down on the chair. "The cottage…" Her voice came out in a whisper, her gaze on the keys.

Mac crossed the space and handed Sophia to Sam before squatting in front of her. "Shawn bought it and was on his way home when he was killed. Mr. Batty put it in your name and when he sent the custody papers he sent those keys. The cottage is yours."

"But I'm staying here."

"I hope so." He took her hands in his. "The cottage belongs to you. It's what your grandmother would have wanted. There will come a day when I retire from the military and we can travel between here and Texas, or anywhere you want, and we can stay at the cottage as much as you'd like. It's also there for when you wish to visit your parents. It's closer than Shawn's house. But no matter what, it belongs to you and should stay in your family. We can rent it out as a vacation cottage if you'd like. From what Mr. Batty was telling me it's beautiful with a creek running close and a lake not far away. People pay good money to get away from it all in places like that."

"The cottage is mine." She'd heard Mac say it but until she said the words herself she didn't believe it. "Grandma's place. Oh, Mac." Tears poured from her eyes and she wrapped her arms around his neck.

"*Amore*, I didn't think this would upset you."

"I'm not upset, I'm just emotional. I love it." She clung to him until the tears stopped falling.

"Grams would want you to have it." Sam's words had her turning to look at him standing there holding both Gabriella and Sophia. "You've always loved that place."

"But I can't enjoy it if I'm here."

"You can enjoy it occasionally and when you're not there someone else can, just as Mac said...a vacation home. You know no one will cherish that place as much as you do," Sam reasoned.

"Or if you want we can sell it, or sell Shawn's house and buy a cottage closer. Somewhere we can slip away to anytime we want. Whatever makes you happy, *amore*."

"We don't need both places." It pained her to say it, even if it was logical. She didn't want to get rid of either place, they were both home. "Maybe we should sell them both. Texas was my home but it isn't any longer. My home is here, with you and the girls."

"What about when you visit your parents?" Mac ran his thumb over her knuckles.

"Let's face it, visits to my parents are going to be few and far between. Mom just doesn't understand what I'm doing with my life and she isn't supportive." She tossed the key in her hand, up and down. "This made sense when I was in Texas, since it was less than an hour drive from Shawn's, but now that I'm here…not so much. With a house full of kids like we've talked about, there's just not enough room in the cottage. If we're keeping it as somewhere to stay when we visit it doesn't make sense. It would be better to keep Shawn's house. There's more room for a large family there."

"No decisions need to be made right now. You can think on it, but right now we need to get to my parents. They'll be expecting us for dinner soon." She let Mac pull her to her feet. "I love you, and if you want all the houses then you shall have them. If you want to sell them, even this one, we'll do it. I want you, Gabriella, and Sophia happy."

"I'm happy with you, and I'm not letting you sell this house. I love it and I want you to finish it." She pressed her body against his and put her arms around his neck. "This is our home." With that she kissed him. It wasn't a timid kiss but one to let him know how much she loved him and cherished that he had given her the cottage. When the kiss ended she needed a moment to collect herself. "Let's get a move on."

She picked up the diaper bag and made her way across to Sam before lifting Gabriella out of his arms. "Mac will take Sophia and you can look at the garage while we put them in their car seats."

"Here're the keys." Mac laid them into Sam's outstretched palm and took Sophia.

With the little girl snuggled against her body, Nicole made her way out of the house and down the steps toward the SUV. Her thoughts were on all the special memories she'd shared at her Grandmother's cottage. So many happy times. As much as she'd wanted it before Shawn had died, she was beginning to think she had to put it behind her. Or at the very least find someone who'd enjoy the cottage as much as Grams and she had. Then, if the time came when Mac retired and they wanted to travel there occasionally, it would be available. The cottage didn't mean as much to her as Mac did.

Love changes everything.

Marissa Dobson

Born and raised in the Pittsburgh, Pennsylvania area, Marissa Dobson now resides about an hour from Washington, D.C. She's a lady who likes to keep busy, and is always busy doing something. With two different college degrees, she believes you're never done learning.

Being the first daughter to an avid reader, this gave her the advantage of learning to read at a young age. Since learning to read she has always had her nose in a book. It wasn't until she was a teenager that she started writing down the stories she came up with.

Marissa is blessed with a wonderful supportive husband, Thomas. He's her other half and allows her to stay home and pursue her writing. He puts up with all her quirks and listens to her brainstorm in the middle of the night.

Her writing buddies Max (a cocker spaniel) and Dawne (a beagle mix) are always around to listen to her bounce ideas off them. They might not be able to answer, but they are helpful in their own ways.

She love to hear from readers so send her an email at marissa@marissadobson.com or visit her online at http://www.marissadobson.com.

Other Books by Marissa Dobson

Alaskan Tigers:

Tiger Time

The Tiger's Heart

Tigress for Two

Night with a Tiger

Trusting a Tiger

Jinx's Mate

Two for Protection

Bearing Secrets

Stormkin:

Storm Queen

Reaper:

A Touch of Death

Beyond Monogamy:

Theirs to Tresure

SEALed for You:

Ace in the Hole

Explosive Passion

Capturing a Diamond

Operation Family

Cedar Grove Medical:

Hope's Toy Chest

Destiny's Wish

Fate Series:

Snowy Fate

Sarah's Fate

Mason's Fate

As Fate Would Have It

Half Moon Harbor Resort:

Learning to Live

Learning What Love Is

Her Cowboy's Heart

Half Moon Harbor Resort Volume One

Clearwater:

Winterbloom

Unexpected Forever

Losing to Win

Christmas Countdown

The Surrogate

Clearwater Romance Volume One

Small Town Doctor

Stand Alone:

Secret Valentine

Restoring Love

The Twelve Seductive Days of Christmas

CPSIA information can be obtained at www.ICGtesting.com
Printed in the USA
LVOW07s1629100515

437948LV00001B/140/P